Twenty Years on Broadway

GEORGE M. COHAN

Twenty Years On Broadway

And the years it took to get there

THE TRUE STORY OF A TROUPER'S LIFE FROM THE CRADLE TO THE "CLOSED SHOP"

By GEORGE M. COHAN

GREENWOOD PRESS, PUBLISHERS
WESTPORT, CONNECTICUT

Originally published in 1925
by Harper & Brothers, Publishers, New York and London

Reprinted with the permission
of Harper & Row, Publishers

First Greenwood Reprinting 1971

Library of Congress Catalogue Card Number 76-138106

ISBN 0-8371-5682-3

Printed in the United States of America

CONTENTS

LIST OF ILLUSTRATIONS

Twenty Years on Broadway

CHAPTER I

HOW IT CAME ABOUT

UNTIL a few minutes ago I had no more idea of ever writing this story than I had of growing a Vandyke beard.

It all came about through my press representative. He asked me to invent an excuse to be handed out to the newspapermen who were besieging my offices for a statement from me concerning my retirement from the play-producing field.

"I've got to tell them something. They've been here every day for a week and you haven't shown up." Dunn said this to me.

Dunn is a "press agent"—the best-dressed "press agent" in the world. Dunn is not only a press agent; he is what is known as a "born press agent," meaning, of course, that his mother told him he was a "press agent" the day he was born.

"Tell 'em I'm busy." It was the only excuse I could think of for the moment.

"Busy doing what?" challenged Dunn. "They know you're not writing a play. You've already declared you were through."

"Tell 'em I'm writing a book."

"What's the name of it?"

"Name it yourself, kid," and away I went to the ball game.

The next morning I picked up a New York paper and read the following:

> George M. Cohan will devote the next three months to a book of reminiscences which will bear the characteristic title of *Twenty Years on Broadway*.

Then followed a story to the effect that Mr. Cohan had decided to keep the world waiting no longer for "the tragic tale of his rapid rise from rags to riches," the publication of which would undoubtedly prove another step forward in the great advancement of American literature.

It was the first hearty laugh I'd had since a certain ex-comic-opera comedian with supposedly strong socialistic ideas confidentially advised me to save my money.

No sooner had I laid down the paper than

the telephone rang. Telephones ring on the "cue" in real life the same as in books and plays.

"What about the serialization of that story you're writing?" An editor of a magazine was speaking.

"Hadn't given it a thought," I answered.

"That's a great title!"

"What is?"

" 'Twenty Years on Broadway'."

"You really think so?"

"What do you think?"

"Hadn't given it a thought," I repeated.

"Well, you ought to; there's something there."

"How much?" I inquired.

"Write your own ticket—I'll be there in twenty minutes to sign the contract."

"Better wait a week or so," I suggested.

"Look here, Cohan, don't string me. Are you writing this story or not?"

"No, I'm not—not yet; but I'm going to start the first chapter just as soon as I hang up this receiver. If you like the darned thing when it's finished, write your own ticket, fix up your contract, and I'll sign it."

"You mean to say that I've given you an idea?" chuckled the editor.

"No, sweetheart," I shot back. "I had the idea; you've given me the courage."

"Go to it, boy!" he shouted.

I hung up, tore off my coat, grabbed a pencil, and went to work.

CHAPTER II

WHAT IT'S GOING TO BE

IT'S going to cramp my style considerably to be compelled to put things in actual writing. Most of my play manuscripts have been mere suggestions of the things I carried in mind. In other words, at least 60 per cent of my playwriting (if you'll permit me to call it that) has been done at rehearsals.

The only person I've ever known who could make head or tail of any manuscript of mine was a young lady stenographer who, after eighteen years of midnight service, got so she could take one peek at any part of my scribbling and translate it into English immediately.

However, during the past month the young lady referred to has allied herself with "other theatrical interests," so here I am, on my own, slowly and carefully putting properly spelled words on paper with nothing to guide me except an unabridged dictionary and a wild desire to "make good" with this editor friend of mine.

My idea in this story is to appeal to the general public. To me the college professor with the tall forehead is of no more importance than the ordinary buck dancer or dramatic critic. My aim is to reach all classes and to be known as the "Mary Pickford of the literary world."

This title of Dunn's, "Twenty Years on Broadway," was all very good from a box-office point of view, but again I wish to state that my style was cramped because a great many things, theatrically, happened to me long before I ever saw the Great White Way, to which the Lambs Club insists that I added the red and blue. You will notice that I have subtitled the story "And the Years It Took to Get There." I did this because I felt it was absolutely necessary to offer a brief *résumé* of my early career (before my name crept into the *Morning Telegraph*), in order to lead up to the mess of work that came after. In so doing, I am not "getting away from my subject," as we say in the Authors League. I am merely edging up to what will doubtless prove to be the most thrilling, daring, and at the same time truthful *exposé* of a "charmed life" ever written by an American song-and-dance man.

CHAPTER III

SCHOOL DAYS AND MUSIC

"GREAT actors are born."

There are many who still doubt the truth of this old saying. But it's a fact. I know, because I was born. Not just ordinarily born, but born on the Fourth of July. (There he goes again.)

I came into the world in a roundabout way. *Via* Providence, Rhode Island. My next birthday will mark my forty-sixth year as a "trouper."

By the time I was three years of age I had screamed my way through several one-night stand routes which my father had personally "booked."

At the age of seven I had grown too big to fit in the top tray of my mother's theater trunk, and yet was too small to be left alone in hotel rooms, so I was shipped back to Providence and placed in the E Street school.

I have learned since that it takes the average scholar from four to five years to go through this school. I was through in six weeks. The principal of the school sent for me and told me so.

"You're through." That's all he said.

The next day I was shipped back to my parents along with a letter which stated that "a few drops of laudanum in beef broth served to the child morning and evening for several days would make the world a safer and saner place to live in." My school days were over.

After six weeks' absence from the show game. I arrived in Boston thoroughly educated and perfectly satisfied that no living man (with the possible exception of John L. Sullivan, who was the champion of the world) could teach me anything more.

My father had just disbanded his "road show," and he and my mother were appearing in a little store on Washington Street in Boston. This store space had been converted into a theater by a man named B. F. Keith. My sister, Josephine, who had also been taken out of school was already in Boston when I arrived. We had a real family reunion that night. Mr. Keith attended the affair and presented Josie with a rag doll, and slipped me a toy balloon.

I learned afterward that B. F. was trying to

jolly my dad into believing that "hard work hurt no man" and that "six performances a day was little enough for any ambitious actor to do."

"You're sure to save money. You can't get outdoors to spend it," said B. F.

"Something in that, too," thought dad.

Keith's business grew to such proportions that he decided to look about for a real theater, and so a little later on we all moved farther up Washing Street to the Bijou. He continued his plan of "continuous performances" and it was in this little house that he started to build the great fame and fortune he left when he died. Mother and dad played there all that season. Josie practiced dancing, high kicking and handsprings. My ambition at that time was to be a black-faced comedian in a comedy musical act.

Dad bought a violin for me and made arrangements with a fiddler friend of his to give me three lessons a week. In two weeks I knew all there was to be known about the violin. The teacher himself said so. He sent me back to my father with a note which read: "Impossible to teach this boy any more. HE KNOWS IT ALL."

CHAPTER IV

ALL KINDS OF JOBS

IN the fall of 1886 I was sent to Orange, New Jersey, and placed in the care of a married couple, friends of my parents. They had no children of their own, so borrowed me to practice on.

Three weeks later, when they were sending me back to my folks, Mr. Higginson, who had escorted me to the station to put me on the train, said, "Tell your father, mother, and sister that we think just as much of them as ever." I saw him jump up and down and throw his hat in the air as the train pulled out.

When I arrived in New York I learned that father, mother, and Josie had just been engaged to play three parts in a Western melodrama called "Daniel Boone on the Trail."

"I don't know what we're going to do with you," said dad. "We can't afford to carry you with the show."

"Why don't you speak to the manager, dad?"

suggested Josie. "There may be something Georgie could do."

"Yes, why don't you do that, Jerry?" added mother.

The next day he brought me to the manager's office, and, as I remember, the whole conversation was about me.

"He's never been on the stage," said dad; "but he's been taking violin lessons, and if I do say it myself, he swings a wicked bow."

"Oh, a fiddler, eh?" The manager began to warm up at this point. "I'll tell you what I'll do, Jerry." He put his hand on father's shoulder as he said this. All managers put their hands on actors' shoulders when they start talking business.

"If the kid will ride the donkey on parade, play second fiddle in the orchestra, and sell song books in the lobby, I'll pay his hotel bills and railroad fares, and you can keep your family intact."

Even at my age (I was eight), and inexperienced as I was in business matters, it seemed to me that this "three-in-one" job that was being handed to me was worth far more than just hotel bills and fares, but dad, not being nearly so good a business man as he was a clog dancer, immediately accepted the proposition, and before we left the office had signed the first contract the Four Cohans ever received.

This "Daniel Boone" show was one of the old-time band-and-orchestra troupes. All the actors had to "double in brass" and sleepers. The star performer was Captain Jack Crawford, the famous poet scout. It was, without doubt, the worst show I ever looked at, and I had to look at it every night from the orchestra pit.

The street parade, however, was one of the best ballyhoos ever perpetrated—cowboys, Indians, wild animals, drum corps, brass band, American flags, and everything else that Barnum ever thought of. I rode the donkey, dad played the bass drum and mother and Josie threw handbills from an old stagecoach that had been discarded by the Buffalo Bill show.

We stayed with this Wild West affair for about six months, and in all that time I never wore anything but a cowboy suit. All the actors in the company had to dress cowboy fashion. We were walking advertisements wherever we went. Before the season was over I got so I even talked like a cowboy. I still do, for that matter.

While with this troupe I developed very fast. The day we left the show (which was on account of a little trouble I'd had with one of the Indians) every member of the company admitted that I had developed. Even the manager told my father that in his opinion "Georgie had developed into the freshest song-book boy in America."

CHAPTER V

FIRST SALARY AS AN ACTOR

"JERRY COHAN'S IRISH HIBERNIA" was the name of a troupe dad organized and started on tour when we finished with "Daniel Boone." With a panorama of Ireland, showing thirty-odd scenes, a couple of Irish bagpipers and a jaunting car, we toured the one-night stands for seven or eight months. My job with this show was driving the two mules hitched to the jaunting car on parade, and taking tickets at the front door, besides selling song books during the intermission.

I got my first experience as an advertising agent with this show. Dad and I used to pass out handbills to the factory hands during the lunch hour, while the Irish bagpipers would drone their jigs and reels. When the "Hibernia" troupe closed, we went back to Keith's (1888). It seemed from that time on that in whatever direction we started, we invariably finished back at Keith's.

This time my father, mother, and a comedian named John Barker formed what became known as the "Bijou Comedy Company." They presented one-act farces, or afterpieces, as they were called then, and gave six performances a day, six days a week, with all-day-Sunday rehearsals thrown in for good measure. They kept this up for six solid months, without any member of the cast missing a single performance.

It was during this engagement that I made my first stage appearance as a boy violinist. It came about in a peculiar way. An act disappointed one Monday morning, and Josie, who had been practicing grotesque dancing for some time, now was rushed in to "fill the gap." Josie made a hit. In fact, a big enough hit to be retained the second week. She was billed as

LITTLE JOSIE COHAN

AMERICA'S YOUNGEST AND MOST GRACEFUL SKIRT DANCER

I wasn't exactly envious of my sister's success, but I must admit that my nose was a bit disjointed and I was bound not to be outdone.

Without my family's knowledge, I had secretly rehearsed myself in a trick violin act, so presented myself to the new general manager whom Mr. Keith had just appointed the week before. The new general manager, by the way, was none other than the same Mr. E. F. Albee who to-day controls the entire high-class vaudeville business of America.

"What kind of an act can you do?" he inquired, after I'd told him how sure I was of "knocking 'em cold."

"I'm a trick violinist," I answered, "and if you'll give me a chance, I'll guarantee——"

Albee interrupted with "What's your salary?" Albee always did come to cases, even in those days.

"I'll make you a fair proposition, Mr. Albee," I went on. "I'll play the week, and you use your own judgment and pay me what you think the act is worth."

"All right. You open next Monday."

I made a dash for the fiddle and practiced several hours a day for the balance of the week. I made my first appearance the following Monday and was billed as

MASTER GEORGIE

VIOLIN TRICKS AND TINKLING TUNES

I finished the week, and Saturday night when I opened my salary envelope I found that it contained exactly six dollars.

"Can you beat that?" I said to a little tenor singer who was dressing with me. "Albee said he'd give me what the act was worth and he hands me six dollars."

"What's the extra dollar for?" he asked.

I made no further "kick."

CHAPTER VI

"THE COHAN MIRTH MAKERS"

THE fiddle went in the prop. trunk. All thoughts of a concert career went smash. For some unknown reason, I suddenly decided to become a drum major, and for several weeks gave all my attention to the art of "swinging the baton."

I managed to book myself at Austin and Stone's Museum for a week's engagement, where I did my juggling specialty and sang a soldier song that went something like this:

I'm Major McPlugg
With the comical mug,
I'm as happy and free
As a bug in a rug.

Through nervousness, the baton got away from me at the opening performance, fled over the footlights, hit the orchestra leader on the head and broke his violin. I squared the fiddle matter all right—I gave him mine.

In the spring of '89, my dad organized our first family road show. The billing matter read:

"THE COHAN MIRTH MAKERS"

The Celebrated Family of Singers, Dancers and Comedians
with their Silver Plated Band
and
Symphony Orchestra

The program ran as follows:

Grand Overture—"Bridal Rose"—
Cohans' Symphony Orchestra
——Mr. and Mrs. Jerry Cohan——
in the clever one-act comedy sketch
"RETIRING FROM THE STAGE"

——Miss Josephine Cohan——
Queen of Terpsichore

——Master George Cohan——
as
"THE LIVELY BOOTBLACK"
—Master Cohan's Own Conception of Buck and Wing Dancing—

——Jerry Cohan——
as
"THE DANCING PHILOSPHER"

—10 Minutes' Intermission—

During which Master Cohan will offer for sale
Autographed Photographs of this fun-creating family

Grand March Selection........Gladiator........Sousa

—THE FOUR COHANS—

in Jerry J. Cohan's Original Comedy with Songs and Dances

"GOGGLES DOLL HOUSE"

concluding with the famous "Dancing Dolls"

Some troupe! Four in the cast, eight in the orchestra. The street parade was the big feature. I was the drum major and led the band of eleven pieces—eight musicians besides the manager, property man and dad. The last three played the snare drum, bass drum, and cymbals. Mother and Josie followed the band in an open victoria draped with American flags. When business was bad we'd discharge the band, cut out the parade, and give the show with a piano player. When business would pick up, we'd hire a new band and begin all over again. No matter what happened, we always carried the trunk of red uniforms, but whether we used them or not was entirely up to the bank roll. We played about six hundred one-night stands with the "Mirth Makers," and during that time we hired and discharged at least half a dozen brass bands. Toward the end of the second season, during one of our bandless periods, the piano went on a spree, so we had to close up altogether and go back to Keith's.

CHAPTER VII

CAST FOR A STAR PART

WE were always welcome at Keith's. I heard B. F. say to my father one day, "It's hard work, Jerry, but it's always here when you want it." (It was now 1891.)

We fooled around, playing variety dates, in the East for several months until we had saved enough capital to put out another troupe. This time it was a three-act farce comedy, written by my father, which he called "Widow McCann's Trip."

It wasn't a very long trip, however, as, during the second week of what was intended to be a tour to the Pacific coast and back, we received a telegram from the Atkinson Comedy Company asking us if we could arrange to open in Brooklyn the following Monday with "Peck's Bad Boy." That was the finish of "Widow McCann." The production went to the storehouse, the actors went back home, and we (the family) went straight to New York and hopped into rehearsals the following evening.

I was the happiest kid in the world. There was I, at the age of thirteen, cast for the rôle of Henry Peck—"that incorrigible lad with a heart of gold," as the program stated. Father and mother played Mr. and Mrs. Peck, and Josie played the bad boy's sweetheart.

We opened Monday matinée to a peanut-eating audience that shrieked with laughter at every move I made. I soaked the grocery-store keeper with a slap stick and they laughed for a full minute. I pushed the Irish policeman into a tub of soap suds, and they stood up and cheered. Mind you, that was over thirty years ago, long before Chaplin had ever tasted a custard pie.

When the matinée performance came to an end I wended my way to the dressing room with the frenzied shouts of approval still ringing in my ears. I was thoroughly convinced that "that guy Booth had nothing on me."

The manager came "back stage" and congratulated my father, mother, and sister. I heard him say to them, "Your individual performances were perfect." I guess he thought I'd get a swelled head if he "boosted" me, so, manager-like, he walked right by my dressing-room door without saying a word.

I was on to his make-believe indifference. I smiled at my reflection in the mirror and had a quiet little talk with myself. "Believe me, you'll pay me, old boy." I was going after the manager to beat the band. "If I play this part next season, you'll pay me, and pay me well."

When I'd finished dressing and had stepped through the stage door into the alley (all stage doors were in alleys in those days) a great shout went up from a band of urchins who not only clogged up the alley, but were also hanging on window sashes and fire escapes in their frantic efforts to get a look at the famous bad boy in the flesh.

"There he is, that's Henry." "There he is," they shouted, as I came through the door.

"Hurray! Hurray! Hurray!"

It was the first big thrill I'd ever known. I was surrounded in a second.

"Three cheers for the bad boy!" cried a dirty-faced enthusiast who, along with a dozen others, was leaning over the roof of the building opposite. He lost his balance, fell off, but grabbed hold of the fire escape, and crawled back to the roof, while the chorus of a hundred voices shouted: "Hurray! Hurray! Hurray!"

I bowed to them very graciously and attempted to find my way through the applauding crowd. I was smiling, shaking hands, and thanking them all over the place. "I'm a hero," I thought to myself.

And then, without any warning, bang! right square on the nose. It was the first real "wallop" I had ever received. Bang! another. This time to the right eye. Before I could get my hands up, bang! an upper cut to the chin.

Bang! Bang! Bang! A million fists came flying in my direction. The hotel was just a hundred yards away from the end of the alley. I did it in nine and four-fifths. Potato spuds kept bouncing off the back of my head the entire distance.

"Oh, my boy! My poor little boy!" cried mother as I ran into her arms in the hotel lobby. The mob of juvenile bandits, still shouting their threats from the sidewalk, made funny faces at me through the plate-glass windows.

"You made a mistake in running away, Georgie," said the manager of the show, who had witnessed my world's-record dash. Then he turned to father.

"This isn't an unusual occurrence at all, Jerry," he went on. "The ambition of every kid in America is to take a punch at Peck's bad boy. Georgie will have to get used to it if he wants to play the part."

He said this very casually, and walked into the dining room without offering any further consolation.

The four of us got together and talked over the advisability of handing in our two weeks' notice.

"What do you want to do, son?" Dad put it up to me.

"I'll stick," I said. "I'll play this part even though I die in the attempt."

The result was that for the following thirty-five weeks I fought my way out of every popular-priced alley on the ten, twenty and thirty-cent circuit.

CHAPTER VIII

TURNING INTO AN AUTHOR

WHEN we left the "Bad Boy" show (which was due to a little trouble I'd had with a crew of stage hands) I had lost more battles than Terry McGovern won in his entire career.

That summer we played the county fairs. We used to go into the "fair towns" and make a deal with the officials to do our specialties on the judges' stand between the heats of the trotting races. The village band supplied the music.

This scheme proved rather profitable, and dad, I remember, was very proud of having thought of the idea.

We saved enough money from the "fair engagements" to promote a new troupe, so the following September (1892) we took to the road again in a three-act farce comedy entitled "Four of a Kind," written, composed, and staged by father.

It was a pretentious production. The scenery alone cost us $450. We carried ten other actors besides the family, and had to play to at least $150 a night to break even.

The answer to this big "overhead" was that we were soon back playing variety dates, and Thanksgiving week found us opening at Robinson's Theater in Buffalo, New York. We were engaged for a single week, but continued on there week after week, putting on sketches, specialties, dancing acts, farces, pantomimes, melodramas, and any other form of entertainment the management called for, until well into the following summer.

During this engagement, I played everything from Boucicault's Irish heroes to black-faced comedy parts. One week I played my own mother's father, mother being cast for the old General's daughter, and I for the General. It was about this time I got the writing bug.

I wrote a one-act play and brought it to dad with the hope that he'd put it on.

"Very good, son; try again." That was all he said, and handed it back.

I tried again and again, but it was always the same set speech, "Try again."

I used to think in those days that father was my severest critic.

I received some remarkably fine press notices while I was playing in Buffalo. There was an advertising weekly, called the Buffalo *Advertiser,* being published there at that time, and through one of the owners of the sheet I got a job soliciting "ads." The understanding was that I was to receive 5 per cent of all moneys derived from the result of my efforts, and besides this I was given a full column space in every issue, which was devoted to eulogizing the performances of "the rising young comedian, George M. Cohan, now appearing at Robinson's Theater." I wrote these notices myself; you can understand how good they were.

Making up my mind that I was not receiving the proper encouragement for my attempts at playwriting, I now turned my attention to the popular-song field. I turned out no less than half a dozen ballads a week for some little time. The New York music publishers must have grown tired of sending back my manuscripts, because after a while they didn't even bother to do that. One fellow, however, was at least courteous enough to write a letter. It ran as follows:

DEAR SIR:

Your songs are not publishable. Please do not send any more.

Even that didn't stop me. As a matter of fact, it made me fighting mad.

"I'll show these guys a few things before I finish. . . . Not publishable, eh? Humph! Well, they'll be published all right. . . . They'll be published if I have to start my own publishing concern and publish them myself." (Business of walking up and down the room, reading the carpet.) "My songs are great. I know they are." (Business of tearing up the publisher's letter.) "Yes, and so are my sketches. . . . Father doesn't think so, but I'll show him a thing or two. . . . I'll write a hundred plays before I'm through. . . . Yes, and they'll be produced, too. . . . They'll be produced if I have to build my own theater, and produce them myself." (Business of going to the window, leaning on the sill and looking into space.) "New York . . . that's the town . . . that's where I belong. . . . I'm sick and tired of wasting my time and talents on these Middle West 'boobs.' " (Business of grabbing hat and rushing out the door, downstairs, and to the street.) "Broadway. . . . Yes, sir! . . . that's where I'm going—to Broadway . . . just as quick as I can. . . . When I get there I'll open my own music-publishing house, build my own theater, and do as I please. . . . Then, thank Heaven, I won't have to listen to any back talk from father or music publishers or anybody else."

These were the thoughts flashing through the mind of "the rising young comedian, George M. Cohan, now appearing at Robinson's Theater," as he sauntered up and down Buffalo's main thoroughfare between matinée and night, flipping the ashes from his Sweet Caporal and looking with utter disdain on the "boobs" as he scornfully passed them by.

CHAPTER IX

WONDERFUL DREAMS

"I THINK it's about time we made up our minds to try for a New York engagement," I said to Dad.

"I think it's about time you understood that you have nothing to say in the matter," he answered, very curtly, and walked away, thereby ending the conversation before it was half started.

That night I packed my belongings into a suitcase.

"All right, if he feels that way about it," I muttered to myself. "Let him stay out here and be a water-tank trouper if he wants to, but there's one member of this family going to tear for Broadway right now . . . to-night. . . . No more kidding about it, either."

I carried on this monologue while throwing the manuscripts of my unproduced one-act plays and unpublished songs in the grip, along with the necessary wearing apparel I had decided to carry. When the packing was completed I sat down and scribbled the following note to my mother:

> Good-by, mother. Don't worry about me. I'm on my way to New York to sell my songs and plays and get a job in a Broadway show. Dad doesn't seem to think that I amount to anything, but keep a-praying for me and everything will come out all right. Please don't let anybody try to bring me back, because my mind is made up to fight it out alone.
>
> Your loving son,
>
> GEORGE.

I intended to slip the note under my parents' door before leaving, figuring that by the time they discovered it there I'd be safe and sound in New York. I had already purchased my transportation and an upper berth on the fast express leaving Buffalo at midnight.

These railroad accommodations, by the way, put quite a dent in my twenty-nine-dollar bank roll, but I knew there was a lot of loose money thrown around Broadway, and I was the little fellow who was going there to pick it up.

Just as I had sealed the envelope and was about to grab for my coat and hat, the door of my room flew open and dad walked in with a broad grin on his face. Dad always grinned when he was nervous.

"Listen, son," he began, "I've been thinking over that matter you spoke of to-day—you know, about New York—and your mother and I have decided to take your tip and go there."

"When are you going?" I asked, impatiently.

"Well, there's no use in starting there this kind of weather. (It was June.) We'll close here in two weeks and then play the summer resorts until late August. That'll bring us to the big town about the first of September."

"You won't get an opening if you wait till September. You've got to be on the ground during the summer to get a job there." I'd heard an acrobat make this assertion, so I pulled it on dad to show him how well I knew the business end of the game.

"Don't worry about a New York opening," he assured me. "Keith's just taken over the Union Square Theater and opens it as a variety house Labor Day week. We're sure of a job with Keith, so you see we'll get a hearing, anyway."

This was all news to me and it sounded reasonable enough to set me turning over in my mind the problem of how to redeem my railroad fare in case I decided to reconsider my "getaway." I stood there trying to think, but my mind was hazy. I glanced hurriedly at my watch. I had fifteen minutes to make the train. I noticed a peculiar look in dad's eyes. He seemed to be studying me.

"Better let me have that railroad transportation of yours, and I'll see if I can get the money refunded." This came out of a clear sky. He said it so calmly, too.

I was stunned. I couldn't reply. How did he know? Was dad a mind-reader?

"Come on, son," he continued, "hand it over."

I stood there transfixed. I couldn't move.

"You don't want to do anything like this," dad went on. "Why, you'd break your mother's heart! Come on, be a regular fellow and forget all about it; and listen, son, the next time you want to run away, you come and tell me about it, and we'll all run away together, the whole four of us. What do you say, boy, eh?"

Tears came to my eyes. When dad saw this he came over to me, patted my shoulder, and said: "It's all right, son, I understand. I was a boy once myself."

I dug for the railroad tickets and handed them

over. I hung my head. I couldn't look up. I was too ashamed. Dad gave me another little pat on the back and said, "Thanks, son," and started toward the door. When he got there he turned around again and changed the subject.

"Oh, I forgot to tell you, George. I watched you from the first entrance to-night and I honestly believe you did the best song and dance you ever did in your life. You're getting to be a good performer, young fellow, sure as you're born. . . . Well, good night, son."

"Good night, dad," I answered.

And he left the room.

I stood there dumfounded, listening to father's fading footsteps as he walked through the hall from my room to his own. I couldn't fathom the thing at all. Where had he got the information?

Later on I learned that the ticket agent from whom I'd purchased my transportation, and to whom I'd talked a little too much about "breaking into Broadway," had smelled a rat and sent word to the theatre that "the Cohan boy would bear watching." I never guessed this at the time. It was all a great mystery.

After several more attempts at trying to figure the matter out, I dismissed it from my mind and

THE FOUR COHANS IN "THE YANKEE PRINCE"

COHAN'S FIRST OPERA HOUSE

began to unpack my grip. I tore up the "good-by" message I'd written to mother, grabbed a pencil and pad of paper, sat down, and started the first act of a mystery melodrama.

I had written several pages of manuscript, when all of a sudden the pencil dropped from my hand and I fell over the table, sound asleep. My dream was all about New York theaters, music-publishing houses, and famous actors and actresses with whom I was hobnobbing along Broadway.

"Surely you know Georgie Cohan." Nat Goodwin was introducing me to Lillian Russell. A voice from behind shouted, "Hello, Georgie! How are you, kid?" and Joseph Jefferson came running up to greet me.

"Hey, George! I left two seats in the box office for you in my name." It was Charlie Hoyt hollering to me from a passing hansom cab.

"When do you start building your new theater, Mr. Cohan?" inquired Roland Reed as he tapped me on the shoulder with his gold-headed cane to draw my attention.

I was just about to recite a new poem I'd written to Sol Smith Russell, when Gilmore's band came marching through Thirty-fourth Street, playing one of my latest tunes, and *the noise woke me up.*

I undressed, said my prayers (asking the good Lord to make my dreams come true), jumped into bed, and slept like a new-born babe till mother brought in the rolls and coffee.

CHAPTER X

NEW YORK AT LAST

THE variety actors in those days tried to get "seashore jobs" during the hot months. We were lucky enough to be booked for the summer (1893) at Rocky Point, Rhode Island. It was one of those old-time clam-bake resorts; at least it was then, I suppose it still is.

The theater, or pavilion, as they called it, was the champion honky-tonk of all the palaces of amusement we ever played. The actors not only set their own scenery, but after it was set were obliged to pull up the curtain, and at the end of the act go "off stage" and drop the curtain down again.

The only incident of any importance that happened to me during the two months we lingered there was that one Monday they ran short of a "sister team," so I had to put on skirts and a blond wig and do a sister song and dance with Josie.

"What'll these fellows think of me?" I protested. But dad merely smiled and said, "Don't talk so much; go on and do the act."

I did the act all right. But it was the only time in my life I ever chewed tobacco. I kept at it all week, too. I wanted every trouper on the bill to understand that I was a 100-per-cent. "tough guy."

The last week in August came 'round and off we went on our merry way to the great New York City, with a contract for a week's engagement at Keith's Union Square Theater.

The family had never played the big town. Dad and mother had appeared there years before as a sketch team, and had also presented melodramas in the cheaper houses, but this was to be the initial New York appearance of the *"Four Cohans."*

Josie was as nervous as a kitten and acknowledged the fact. On the contrary, I was never so sure of "knocking 'em cold" as I was the Sunday evening before our Union Square opening.

Dad and I went out to take a stroll after supper. We wanted to talk over a few minor changes we were making in the act.

The act was to be "Goggles Doll House," a skit we had played for several years, but father had been working and improving on it and we all felt that he had made it into a 50-per-cent better farce than it ever was before.

"We'll be a 'riot' to-morrow, dad," I said, as I took my first good look at the bright lights of Broadway.

"Don't be too sure, son. You never can tell." My father's lack of confidence, as I figured it to be then, got me nervous and I came back with:

"Well, what's going to stop us? It's the best four act in the business. We know that, don't we? Mother and you have all that sure-fire dialogue. You'll 'murder' 'em with that. Josie's the best dancer in America. We know that, don't we? And as for myself, well——"

I was just about to explain to him, for the thousandth time, what a perfectly marvelous performer I was, and what I would do to this wise metropolitan audience, and how easily I was going to take my rightful place with the high lights of the theater world, when he interrupted me by whispering to me:

"Nix, son. You're talking too loud. Everybody in the street is listening to you."

I hadn't realized it, of course, but I had become so excited and enthusiastic that I was unconsciously shouting all this at the top of my voice, much to the amusement of the hangers-on along the Rialto.

"These Broadway fellows will think you're crazy." Dad fussed with his watch chain. Dad always fussed with his watch chain when he was embarrassed.

"What do I care about these Broadway guys!" As I said this I threw a nasty look in the direction of "the curbstone brigade" in front of the Coleman House.

"I'll fold this street up and put it in my pocket before I get through." I added this loud enough for the "gang" to hear, and a roar of laughter sent father around the corner toward Sixth Avenue.

I followed him with, "What's the idea of the side street?"

"What's the idea of your making a monkey of yourself? Listen, son," he went on, "you'll never get anywhere in this town if you carry on like this. People won't like you; they'll hate you. Anyone, to hear you talk, would put you down for a 'small-headed' kid. It's just as easy to make friends as enemies, and you'll find that friendship is a very necessary thing if you remain in this business. Now please, son, I beg of you, come down to earth. Don't shout so, quit bragging, and put your hat on straight." (I wore it cocked to the side.) "And for Heaven's sake stop juggling that cane." (I carried a switch cane.) "Be human, be yourself, and, damn it all, take that gum out of your mouth. You've been chewing on it for an hour."

Dad was upset, I could see that, so I walked along without a word. By the time we reached the boarding house he had "laid down the law" to a fare-thee-well.

I finished the evening in the folks' room by making all sorts of promises to behave myself from that time on. I swore I'd be "a little gentleman" at the music rehearsal the following morning, and finally retired to the hall bedroom to which I'd been assigned, pulled out one of the bureau drawers, laid it over my lap in desk fashion, reached for the pad and pencil, and started to write an "ad" for the New York *Clipper* (which was then the leading theatrical publication).

The flash headline read:

THE FOUR COHANS TAKE NEW YORK BY STORM

CHAPTER XI

EARLY DISAPPOINTMENTS

"OH, hello Jerry! Glad to see you."

It was the house manager speaking as he shook hands with dad when we entered the stage door of the Union Square Theater the following morning.

"I've just received a telegram from Boston headquarters," he continued. "Here, read it yourself," and he handed the message to dad. Mother, Josie, and I leaned over his shoulders, and we all read it at the same time:

Tell Cohan family not to do the four act. Mr. and Mrs. Cohan in sketch and two children in single turns better for New York audience.

I won't say that we were disappointed. Half paralyzed is a better description.

"This is a big mistake," said dad. "Why, we've been rehearsing the four act night and day for weeks."

"Sure we have. It'll be a sensation, too." I added this.

"Keep quiet, son," my mother snapped.

"Yes, let papa settle it, Georgie." And Josie, as she said this, gave me the high sign to "play dead."

Dad gave me another warning look and then continued to the manager:

"I wish you'd reconsider this switch, Jim."

"It isn't up to me, old pal," he answered. "You know Albee and you know he runs his business to suit himself. I wouldn't give it another thought if I were you. Just go ahead and do the sketch and two singles, and maybe later in the season you'll get a week here for the four act."

"What do you think, Nellie?" Dad put it up to mother.

She advertised her disappointment with a shrug of the shoulders.

"I think this is a crime," I blurted.

"I'll commit one in a minute if you don't keep quiet," said dad.

And Josie started high-signing me again to quit "butting in."

"Well, I dare say the only thing to do is to do as we're told." There was a sad note in dad's voice as he reluctantly murmured this.

He had rewritten the four act completely since we'd last played it, and had great hopes of its being our first big hit. We had gone through a final rehearsal of the thing that morning before we left the boarding house, and were all enthusiastic over the changes and the big chance it had. I knew my single turn wasn't any too strong, so the thing was a double disappointment to me.

"Well, never mind, Jerry. Everything happens for the best," the manager remarked as dad handed back the telegram.

"I suppose so," he replied, without any further resistance except to pucker his lips.

"You mean to tell me you're going to stand for this?" I shouted.

For an answer dad gave me another hard look and I kicked a rosin board clean across the stage and walked to the back door and out to the alley.

"They can't do this to me, I won't stand for it," I started telling it to the world soon as I hit the open air.

"What seems to be the trouble, cutie?" a transfer man inquired as he passed me with a trapeze trunk on his back.

"I wasn't talking to you," I snarled at him.

"Well, I wouldn't make any political speeches around here if I were you. Somebody's liable to poison you." And he disappeared through the stage door, laughing his head off as he went.

I walked to the corner of Fourth Avenue and Fourteenth Street and leaned against a lamp-post, and gave Keith and Albee a "laying out" such as they never heard in all their days. When I'd finished giving them their right names and addresses, I started breaking matches into halves and chucking them in the gutter. I destroyed the entire box and then started the encore to my tirade.

"All right, I'll go in and do the single turn if you want it, but you two guys can understand right now that I'll get even. . . . Yes, sir! . . . I'll get even if I have to spend the rest of my life in taking the roofs of your theatres from over your heads." That was the finish of my verbal assault on the two great managers as I stood there talking to the lamp-post.

I turned back through the alley and walked in the stage door, and discovered dad at the footlights, rehearsing the music of my single turn, "The Lively Bootblack." Mother and Josie were standing to one side, drying their eyes and trying to smile as they saw me coming.

"You ought to rehearse your own music, George. Dad doesn't know your tempos very well," Josie suggested in a stage whisper.

"Yes, I think you should, son," mother added.

I didn't want to appear to be weakening too quickly, so I carried along the bluff.

"I haven't made up my mind yet whether I'll play the week or not."

Dad heard this, looked up, and called to me: "Come on, son, get at this. Rehearse it yourself. Hurry, too. Do you hear?" He didn't say it very gently, either, and when dad didn't say things very gently, it was just as well to give him his own way.

"All right, dad," and I walked to the footlights. Father, mother, and Josie went to unpack the trunks.

When I had rehearsed for about fifteen minutes (five minutes was the allotted time), I leaned over and said to the piano player:

"Now, if you won't mind, we'll just take the whole act right over again and get it down pat."

"Say, how much longer are you going to keep this thing up? There are two or three other acts to rehearse yet. We've got to open these doors at 11.30." The stage manager of the house said this as he came toward me with a broom in his hand. All stage managers did their own sweeping in those days.

"I can't help that," I answered. "I've got to get these tempos right."

"Say, listen!" It was the first time I'd heard the piano player's voice. I had done all the talking up to then.

"If you think I'm going to sit down here and go over that junk again, you're crazy," and then, by way of adding insult to injury, he stood up and yelled, "Anybody would think this guy was rehearsing Hanlon's 'Fantasma,' the way he's been raving around here."

"Where do you get off, to give me any argument?" I shouted back at him. "I've been in this business since I was a child in kilts; Keith can tell you that himself." And then, leaning over the footlights and shaking my finger at him defiantly, I added: "You better go and take a few piano lessons before you start telling me where I get off."

The ushers, all ready in their uniforms, waiting for the house to open, came running down the aisles to hear the argument.

"Look here, Shakespeare"—the stage manager grabbed me by the arm as he spoke—"whatever you do, don't lose your temper, because the last buck dancer that got excited around here had to be buried by the Actors' Fund."

By this time several performers and the entire stage crew had gathered about me in a circle, and all seemed to be enjoying the stage manager's "wise-cracking" remarks.

"You'll get rich kidding me." I was too angry to think of anything clever to say, so I shot this at him. "I'm an artist, I am. I'm too smart to go around the country having arguments with piano players and stage hands."

"Hey, Bill!" the stage manager shouted to one of the crew. "Get that loving cup out of the property room and slip it to this guy. Maybe that'll cure him."

Another loud laugh from the circle.

"I'll have all you guys working for me some day, see if I don't." I half mumbled this, but they heard it and laughed louder than ever.

"We're all going to work for him. Hurray for our new boss!" yelled the property man, and a loud roar went up as father shoved his way through the circle and made a grab for me.

"What's the matter? What's happened?" dad inquired. It seems he'd heard the rumpus from the dressing room where he'd been laying out the wardrobe. "What's happened?" he repeated. "What's the fuss?"

"It's all right, Mr. Cohan," explained the stage manager. "I was just trying to make the boy understand that this theater had to be opened some time this season, that's all."

Dad looked at me. "What was it, son?" he asked.

"Oh, this guy is one of those back-stage comedians," I answered, indicating the stage manager. "He thought I was a 'hick,' I guess."

The stage hands, giggling and exchanging their private opinions of me, moved away and went about their various duties. Another act started to rehearse, and the stage manager, seeing that dad was nervous and upset over the incident, leaned over and said to him:

"I'm sorry this happened, Mr. Cohan; on the level I am. I guess the kid's a little over-anxious, that's about the size of it," and he started to sweep the stage.

"Come on. I want to talk to you right now," commanded dad as he led the way to the dressing room. I followed him; I was gritting my teeth, too.

"Sit down on that trunk there and listen to me." He said this after he had closed and bolted the door.

I did as I was told. I figured I was in for a genuine tongue lashing (the only kind of punishment I ever received from my parents), because I don't believe I had ever seen him quite so angry as he was at that particular moment. I knew I had to think fast to kill off the lecture, and that's what I'd been doing all the way to the dressing room.

"Before you say a word, dad, I want to tell you something," I ventured. "I lost my head, and I'm sorry for it. The stage manager was right when he said he thought I was overanxious. That's what's the matter with me. I'm so dead crazy to make good here in New York that I can hardly think straight. I'll apologize to the piano player, to the stage hands, and everybody else in the theater if you want me to. I was wrong and I admit it. A fellow can't be any more reasonable than that. Nothing of the kind will ever happen again, dad, I give you my word," and as I said this I stood up and extended my hand to him.

He weighed me up for a moment before he spoke, and then he asked, "I can positively rely on that?"

"Positively."

"No more outbursts?"

"Not a chance."

"No kick of any sort from now on?"

"I'm through kicking, dad, once and for all."

"All right, son, then we'll let it go at that."

We shook hands, and I started to hang up my "Lively Bootblack" specialty clothes. A knock came at the door.

"Just a second," shouted dad. He unbolted the latch, and a boy in uniform looked in the room with a "time sheet" to tell us where we were on the bill.

"Is Master George Cohan in here?" he inquired, as he referred to the paper to get the name correct.

"Right here," I answered.

"You're on 'number one.' You open the show," he said as he checked me off with a pencil dash.

"I what?" I fairly screamed this.

"You open the show," he repeated, and disappeared down the hall, calling out the names of various performers and acquainting each one with his or her spot on the program. If the theatre building had caved in it couldn't have buried me any deeper than I was right then. Josie was "spotted" fourth, mother and dad sixth. I was to "open" the show. Dad stood in the center of the room, waiting for the explosion. It came, with a bang!

"They can't do this to me. I won't be disgraced by these guys. I'd rather be a tramp in the gutter than stand for this." They heard me hollering throughout the entire building. I meant that they should.

"Now, don't take on like that, son. Remember the promise you just made." Dad tried to make this sound like a command, but there was a note of pity in his voice, just the same.

"What do they think I am around here—a Patsy Bolivar?" I yelled.

Mother and Josie came running into the room and tried to console me, but I tore up and down like a madman, calling Keith and Albee everything on the calendar. Dad, mother, and Josie stood by, watching this performance with both fear and sympathy registered on their faces. For several minutes I raved and ranted, and finally threw myself on top of a trunk and wept bitter tears.

"Please don't take it so to heart, son." My mother was having a little cry herself as she said this to me.

"What'll that gang in Buffalo think when they hear about this?" I bellowed as the family gathered about me.

"If Georgie feels that way about it, let's not play the engagement at all. Let's all quit and be done with it." This was Josie's suggestion.

"That satisfies me," put in dad. "If your mother's agreeable," and he looked in her direction for the decision.

"Perhaps that would be the easiest way out of it," she said, and began to bathe my forehead with witch hazel.

At this point the call boy shouted through the hall: "Curtain up in ten minutes. Everybody dressed, please!" I jumped from the trunk.

"I'll go through with it," I hollered as I started tearing off my street clothes. "I'll go through with it and make them all ashamed of themselves. Mark my words, before the week is over I'll be in the middle of this bill. See if I won't. I'll go out there and knock that audience 'into a cocked hat,' that's what I'll do. I'll dance like I never danced in all my life. I'll turn this defeat into victory" (a line from one of the plays I had written). I raised my right hand above my head and pointed to the ceiling as I shouted this. "They can't discourage or dishearten me—no, siree. I just won't be licked. I'll show this New York public a few things they've never seen before. Oh, I'll open the show. Yes, I'll open the show" (this half hysterically) "and God help the acts that follow me, that's all I've got to say." I shouted this threat at the top of my voice so every performer on the bill could hear it. Mother and Josie ran out of the room. Dad did the best he could to assist me in the hurried preparations for my big city début. I hopped into my specialty make-up, grabbed my bootblack box, threw it over my shoulder, and made for the door. When I got there I turned and shouted a parting threat at my father, "I'll get even with Keith and Albee, see if I don't." And I rushed to the stage.

CHAPTER XII

MY FIRST NEW YORK AUDIENCE

"IS your act very noisy?" a stage hand inquired as I stood in the first entrance, waiting for the pianist to play the people into their seats.

"What do you mean, is my act very noisy?"

I felt that I was being "kidded," and half realized that it was because of the exhibition of temper I had displayed at the music rehearsal.

"Well, I just want to put you wise," he went on. "Those people out front have probably been up all night and they're here to get a good sleep, so if there's any noisy stuff in your act, I'd advise you to cut it out, because if you wake them up they'll hiss you."

He said this in a very confidential way, and then walked away whistling "My Sweetheart's the Man in the Moon," which was the popular song of the day and at which the piano player out front was banging away in his medley overture. As this stage hand walked away, another fellow came over to me.

"Remember, kid," he whispered, "you're playing to a lady audience in this house. No rough stuff, no blue jokes or anything else like that. We won't stand for it here."

I was the "Humpty Dumpty." I realized it at once. I started to turn away, and bumped into the property man, who was standing behind me with a "prop. gun" in his hand.

"Here you are, kid," he said, as he offered the weapon to me. "Stick that in your kick, and if that piano player doesn't get your tempos right, shoot him dead before you leave the stage."

"Hey! Lay off that fellow! What are you guys trying to do, get him nervous? Let him alone. Can't you see he's got stage fright already?" The stage manager said this as he came up and shooed the rest of the crew away. Then he turned to me. "Don't you mind them, Georgie," he said. "Go on there and show that bird Augustin Daly that you're just as good a performer as he heard you were."

"Augustin Daly? Is he out front?" I asked, half believing it was true.

"Sure he's out front. He's standing up in the rear, disguised as a policeman. He sent word "back stage" not to let you know, but I'm tipping you off because I've taken a great liking to you."

It suddenly dawned on me that he was about as sincere as the others.

"You'll get rich trying to string me." For the second time that morning, it was all I could think of to say. They had me "going," all right, but I pretended not to mind their banter, so threw a knowing smile at the stage manager and strolled to the back wall and started "limbering up." I was trying to get my bearings. I got thinking again about the great injustice of putting me on to open the show, and was giving Keith and Albee another good "talking to," when suddenly I heard the introductory strain to my opening number and I rushed down to the first entrance and on the stage.

"I'm called the Lively Bootblack
  For my style and occupation,
When work is done I like to play
  By way of recreation.
My cousin is an actor boy;
  He's often been before you;
I know you're fond of dancing,
  So a specimen I'll show you."

Then into an Irish reel. NOT A HAND. The last four lines of the second verse ran:

> "I sneaked into a fancy ball
> With whiskers made of false hair.
> The dancers couldn't dance at all;
> I taught them how to waltz there."

Then into a waltz clog. NOT A HAND. I then recited "The Bootblack's Dream," a dramatic story in rhyme about a "he" Cinderella. NOT A HAND. And then this announcement:

"Ladies and gentlemen, I will now offer for your approval my own conception of the most difficult form of the terpsichorean art, commonly known as buck-and-wing dancing. I wish to call your particular attention to the fact that the steps are of my own invention and that no other living dancer has ever been able to master the same routine."

After this modest speech I said to the piano player, "If you please, Professor," and into the dance, finishing with a run up either side of the proscenium arch, back to center stage, and a break and bow. NOT A HAND.

No response of any kind from the thirty-five or forty persons seated in front. As a matter of fact, at least a dozen of them had been reading newspapers throughout my entire act. At one point during the recitation of "The Bootblack's Dream," one woman commenced to giggle and the rest of the audience hushed her up, but that was the only sign of life they showed during the ten minutes I occupied the stage.

I bowed at the end of the dance, and the piano player "tremoloed" a sustained chord to take me off. I walked to the first entrance, bowed again, and made my exit in absolute silence.

"You paralyzed 'em, kid, you killed 'em. They're all dead out there." One of the stage hands said this as I passed him on the way to the dressing room where the other members of my family were waiting to hear the result of my New York triumph. In those days the performers had to remain in their dressing rooms until called for their acts.

"How did you go, son?" asked dad eagerly, as I rushed in with my jaw set and fire in my eyes. He asked the question before he realized my frame of mind.

"I'll get even with Keith and Albee for this, if it's the last thing I ever do." As I made this statement I threw the bootblack box the full length of the room. It struck a water pitcher on a table in the corner and, *crash* the thing splintered and flew all over the floor.

"Hey! Cut that out!" came a voice from the hall outside, and the house fireman rushed in to see what had happened. Mother and Josie ran out of the room, and dad started picking up the broken pieces of crockery.

"What are you trying to do—put this theater on the blink?" As the fireman said this he backed me against the wall of the dressing room to make sure of no further damage being done.

"Oh, don't worry, I'll pay for it," I sulked.

"You can bet your life you'll pay for it," he answered as he pinned my arms to my sides. "And say, listen. Just one more move out of you and I'll—"

"Never mind, Tom, I'll handle this," interrupted the house manager, who ran into the room at this point. "Don't bother about that, Jerry. I'll have it swept up," he said to dad, who was still gathering together the broken bits of the pitcher. Then he turned to me.

"Come outside a minute. I want to talk to you," and he beckoned me out of the room. The fireman released his hold on me and I followed the manager to the hallway. He took me by the arm and started walking me up and down.

"Of course, it's none of my business," he began as we stepped along, "but you're making a big mistake, young fellow. You're not treating your folks right. Do you know that? If you keep on acting up like this you'll just worry them to death. Your mother and sister are both hysterical already, and look at your dad in there. He's just about sick over it all. What's the matter with you, anyway? Haven't you any feeling for your own people?"

I didn't answer. I couldn't. I was too ashamed.

"Will you take my advice and do as I tell you?" he continued.

"What do you want me to do?" I asked.

"I want you to go in there to your father and apologize. Tell him you're sorry about the way you've carried on here to-day, and promise him faithfully that it will never happen again." The fact that I'd made this very promise less than half an hour before struck me on the funny bone, my sense of humor got the better of me, and I began to smile.

"What are you grinning about?" inquired the manager.

"I can't help it; it's funny."

"What's funny?"

"Everything," and I started snickering.

"Gee! you're a tough kid." As he said this he shook his head hopelessly and started to walk away. I followed him down the hall.

"No, I'm not a tough kid; there's nothing tough about me at all." He stopped to listen to my argument.

"I'm just human, that's all," I went on. "I stand up for my rights the same as you or anybody else. I'll admit that I lose my temper, but so does every other regular fellow once in a while. I'm not getting an even break, that's what's the matter. I never kick unless I've got a kick coming to me. I don't want to worry my folks. I think as much of my folks as anybody in the world does, but everything's wrong around here. Everybody's against me."

"Who's against you?" he challenged.

"Everybody," I shot back.

"Who's everybody?" he tried to stump me.

"Oh, Keith and Albee, and everybody else. If you ask me, I think I've been treated pretty rotten by the whole outfit."

The manager, who up to now had treated

the matter seriously, suddenly broke into a fit of laughter, and several performers whose heads had been stuck out of dressing-room doors, listening to the conversation, joined in the merriment. Finally, mother, dad, and Josie came into the hall, caught the spirit of the thing, and inside of thirty seconds the whole affair was turned into a free-for-all laughing contest.

I rushed into my dressing room, slammed the door, and walked up and down the floor, "taking it out" on the world in general. After a few seconds I stood still and listened. The laughter not only continued, but had increased tenfold. The darned thing was so contagious that, to tell the truth, as hard as I tried not to, I was finally compelled to laugh a little myself.

I hurriedly dressed for the street, ran around the corner, bought an admission ticket, and stood out front and watched my sister Josie make a genuine hit.

"That's what a good spot on the bill will do," I muttered to myself as I walked over to Union Square and leaned against the lamp-post.

CHAPTER XIII

ENEMIES AT WORK

IT won't be necessary to go into details of what happened during the balance of the Union Square engagement. The attitude of the people about the theater was very much "upstage" so far as I was concerned. As soon as I noticed this fact I was smart enough to stay in the background and sort of hide away.

The stage hands kept at me, however, and referred to me as "Young Henry Irving" and whispered wise cracks in my ear every chance they got. Most of the performers on the bill passed me up without a word; one or two of them "kidded" me in a mild way, while a few others, taking pity on a spoiled boy, tried to jolly me along with a friendly smile now and then.

I tamed down considerably after Monday matinée—so much so, in fact, that by the middle of the week I was in the shrinking violet class.

Through the entire eighteen consecutive performances (three a day), 12.05, 5.20, and 7.25 P.M., I continued to "die standing up," as they used to say when an act failed to score a hit. The hours of my appearances were such that I never saw over a baker's dozen sitting out front, until my final performance Saturday evening. I peeked through the first-entrance draperies before I went on, and saw that the house was packed.

"Here's where I get a real chance at these babies," I said to myself as I dashed on and into my opening song.

It was what was known as an over-friendly Saturday-night "set up" audience. They started laughing at the box office when they bought their tickets.

My Irish reel got a round of applause. The waltz clog went well enough to take an encore.

"Ah, ha! I'm even at last," the thought flashed through my mind. "Keith and Albee tried to ruin me, but the little old Rhode Island kid will finish the week in a blaze of glory." No one on earth could have bought that bootblack box from me for a million dollars at that particular moment.

All the old self-assurance that had deserted

me during the week came back with a rush. I had the New York public in the palm of my hand. I told a couple of jokes which I added for this occasion, and got two great big laughs. The act was going along like a house on fire. I went into my recitation, "The Bootblack's Dream," absolutely convinced that I'd "murder 'em" with that, but just as I got to the most dramatic part (where the kid falls asleep on the doorstep and starts dreaming that he's the rich man's son) a couple of fellows in the gallery got into an argument, started a fight, and the entire audience stood up and gave its undivided attention to the "battle royal" which it developed into when the house policeman tried to stop the bout.

My heart sank into my dancing shoes, but I kept right on reciting just the same.

An American crowd would rather look at a prize fight any time than the best show on earth. They proved the fact right then. At least, I thought they did.

The noise was deafening, but I kept right on reciting. No one out front was paying the slightest attention to me at all, with the exception of the piano player, who had it in for me anyway, so he sat there laughing his head off as I hollered myself hoarse trying to make them hear what I was reciting about.

"Go on. Soak him in the eye, Mickey!"

"Upper-cut him in the mush, Red!"

"Cheese it! Here comes the cop!"

"Let 'em alone, you big bum! Let 'em fight it out!"

The house was in an uproar. I saw there was no use, so I cut short the recitation.

"Go into the dance," I shouted to the piano player. His back was turned to me now; he was looking at the fight himself.

"Go into the dance," I yelled again. This time he heard me, so swung himself around on the stool to the keyboard and went into the buck-and-wing music while I threw the jig sand from one end of the stage to the other and started my routine. Two or three other gallery fights had begun by this time, much to the delight of the laughing and applauding crowd that stood in a body, backs turned to the stage, shouting their comedy instructions to the various contestants above.

I kept right on dancing. No one was looking at me, but I kept on dancing just the same. I added steps, repeated steps, invented steps, and "hoofed" myself blue in the face trying to get their attention, but all in vain. What I called Keith and Albee and the stage hands and the monkey-faced piano player during all this would send me to Atlanta if I put it on paper.

By the time the theater "cop," assisted by two other officers of the law, called from the outside, had dragged the offenders from their seats and out through the gallery door, I was weak in the knees from the endurance dance I had been doing.

The thing that hurt me more than anything else, I remember, was the thought that the piano player with the silly grin on his face was having the time of his life getting "hunk" with me. I finished with the regulation "break" in the center of the stage, bowed, and started to walk off while the audience, still laughingly discussing the gallery fight and ruffling programs, began to resume their seats without knowing who was bowing, why I was bowing, or what it was all about. It was the toughest ordeal I'd ever been through. I was sure the whole world was against me. I was puffing like a steam engine.

"I've played many a dump in my time, but

this is the 'champ' of them all." I made this declaration loud enough for everybody back stage to hear, as I stalked through the first entrance, headed for the dressing room.

"Say, listen, kid. That was a rotten trick they played on you out there to-night. It was all spite work and I can prove it if you want me to." The property man said this as he caught up with me and walked along to the rear of the stage.

"What do you mean, spite work?" I inquired.

"Why, that scrap in the gallery was started simply to put your act on the bum," he pointed out. "I've got the dope. I heard the whole thing 'cooked' up. I know the two guys that started the thing and I also know that they were planted there purposely to kill your act."

"Who were they?"

"Keith and Albee," he whispered. "They went up there disguised as a couple of Spaniards, and pulled the whole thing off just to get even with you for taking money for that act you did here this week."

He said all this very hurriedly without cracking a smile, and then walked away, whistling to himself as happy as a lark. As cruel a thing as it was to say, I remember that I couldn't help admiring the fellow for his sense of comedy as I watched him walk across the stage. I continued on my way to the dressing room, and when I got there dad handed me a telegram he had just received, which read as follows:

> Can book Josephine Cohan for single dancing specialty at Koster and Bial's, opening Monday night. Salary same as Four Cohans are receiving jointly from Keith.

The message was signed by James J. Armstrong, who was one of the big variety agents of New York City. I read it over and burned under the collar.

"What do you think of it?" asked dad, knowing fairly well that it didn't come under the head of good news to me.

"I think it's an insult, that's what I think of it, and Armstrong ought to be ashamed of himself for ever having sent such a telegram." And I threw it on the make-up shelf to register my indignation.

"But it's the same salary the four of us are getting here," argued dad.

"Yes? Is that so? Well I'm not letting any woman support me. I want that understood now and forever." That ended the discussion for the time being.

Dad started making up for his act, and I began packing my trunk.

"I hope I never have to play this joint again," I mumbled to myself as I threw my stage clothes in the top tray.

I couldn't get the gallery fight out of my mind at all.

A few minutes later, while I was spreading cocoa butter over my face to remove the grease paint, I got to thinking about Koster and Bial again, and gave them a "dressing down" that must have made their ears burn. In my estimation, from that moment on they were in a class with Keith and Albee.

Dad never uttered a word during all this monologue; he merely started humming to himself. Dad always used to start humming when he wanted to control his temper.

CHAPTER XIV

MIXING IN WITH THE STARS

THE next morning (Sunday) Josie and I were called to our parents' room, and the four of us went into conference about the Koster and Bial offer. Koster and Bial's music hall at that time was the leading high-class vaudeville theater of America. At least, it was so far as the variety actors were concerned.

The agent's office had sent word that they would have to know our decision immediately regarding Josie's appearance there, as the engagement was to begin the following night.

Much to my surprise, Josie herself very diplomatically took my side of the argument, which was that the arrangement would not only professionally belittle the other members of the family, but would also destroy the trade mark of the "Four Cohans." Had she shown the slightest sign of being in favor of the engagement, or had I imagined for a moment that there was any inclination on her part to accept the offer, they never in the world would have managed to bring me around to the "dollar-and-cent" way of thinking.

Josie used to say this about me, "Give my brother his own way about anything, and he'll do it your way nine times out of ten."

That's pretty good "dope" on any stubborn person, and the system has proved valuable to me on several occasions.

After a pretty "peppery" discussion, it was finally settled that Josie was to accept the Koster and Bial proposition, so dad sent word around to the agent's office that everything was O.K.

After her opening performance she was engaged indefinitely. (She was a heavenly dancer.) She was also immediately booked at what was known then as the Vaudeville Club, which was a sort of society cabaret affair over the Metropolitan Opera House. This double engagement lasted for weeks and weeks. Later in the season she was transferred to the Imperial Music Hall, which afterward became Weber and Fields' playhouse. She rounded out the entire winter as a single-handed entertainer at twice the salary the "four" had ever received.

During her Imperial engagement I said to

her one day, "Why don't you speak to the manager of that house and see if you can't get him to put me on for my single specialty?"

"I'll speak to him about it to-night, Georgie."

The next day she brought what she thought was good news.

"Everything's fixed, George," she said. "I've arranged for you to show your act." I was tickled pink. "There's to be a big benefit performance at the Imperial Friday afternoon," she went on. "It's to raise money for the yellow-fever sufferers in the South. All the big stars of the town are going to appear, and Mr. Krauss told me that he'd be only too glad to look at your specialty if you care to go in the bill."

"I don't think so much of that idea," I said, disappointedly.

"Well, at least it's a hearing," put in dad.

"Why don't you do it, son?" chimed mother.

"What does that guy think I am—a benefit actor?" And to emphasize my contempt for the idea I added, "He's just trying to get something for nothing, that's what he's doing."

After thinking the matter over that night, however, I decided that it might be well to break into a big all-star bill even at a benefit performance, so the next morning I went to Josie and told her to inform the manager that I would positively appear if he'd give me a good spot on the program. She came back that same night with the information that no particular time or spot could be promised, but that the curtain was to rise at 1.30 and the bill would probably run until well after 5.30. If I cared to come there and take a chance, they'd put me on whenever they could.

"Oh, just want to use me for a convenience, is that the idea?" When I "pulled" this speech, dad, mother, and Josie, all three, walked away and left me flat.

Regardless of the indignant stand I'd taken about the benefit offer, I could hardly wait for Friday to come. The curtain was advertised to rise at 1.30 P.M. I was there at 12.30, bootblack box and all. I missed the music rehearsal at 9.30 in the morning, as no one had notified me when it was to take place.

I got hold of the house musical director, however, and gave him my song arrangements and explained the act and the tempos to him as best I could.

"Now, be very careful and keep the string in-

GEORGE M. COHAN IN "APRIL FOOL"

LITTLE JOSIE COHAN

struments muted during my recitation," I explained, "and tell your cornet player to come along with the melody of the repeat chorus as forte as he can in the opening song."

"All right," he said, and started to go; but I grabbed him again.

"And listen, Professor," I continued, "ask the drummer to give me a long 'roll' on the snare drum when I finish the buck-and-wing dance. Look, here's the step I do for the climax." And I went through the mechanics of the thing to illustrate. His mind seemed preoccupied. He kept looking around in thirty directions during all this explanation. He started away again and I grabbed him the second time.

"Just one thing more," I started. And he pulled away from me and shouted:

"For God's sake, shut up! I've got forty acts on my mind. You could explain all this in two minutes; you've taken a quarter of an hour already."

"Oh, you're one of those guys that know it all, is that the idea?"

"Say, who is this person, anyway?" he turned and inquired of one of the stage hands. Josie walked through the back door at this point, and, instinctively feeling that I was in a "jam," as usual, came running over in our direction. She explained to the musical director that I was her brother, and went on to say how thankful she'd be if he could assist me in any way at all.

"I'll do the best I can for him, Miss Cohan," he said, "but he's been annoying the life out of me for the last fifteen minutes." He glanced at his watch. "I've got to get out front and start the overture; I'm late now." And he dashed downstairs, headed for the orchestra pit.

"You should be more careful how you talk to people, Georgie," Josie warned me.

"Where do you get off, to tell me what to do?" I returned. "Nobody's paying me anything for this performance. I'm doing it for nothing."

"So is everybody else," she shot back.

"Ask that stage manager what time I go on, will you, please?"

"Ask him yourself," she snapped, and walked to her dressing room. Josie was frightfully disturbed, and showed it, too.

I waited around the stage for a couple of hours, listening to round after round of hearty applause received by all the celebrated artists appearing before an audience that packed the little music hall from pit to dome.

I remember following Ned Harrigan from one side of the stage to the other in order to get a look at him. I mixed in here and there with different groups that carried on "shop-talk" conversation, and kept moving about in a sort of half-interested, half-disgruntled way, wondering where and when I'd be put on the bill.

About 4.30 I walked down to the first entrance, pushed my way through the crowd, and tugged at the stage manager's coat tail.

"Will you please tell me what time I go on?" I asked.

"What's your name?" he inquired.

"George M. Cohan," I replied.

"Don't know anything about it," he answered.

"Well, who does know? Who's running this gag, anyway?"

"Don't bother me now," he said. "I'm busy." And he started waving his hand to some performer on the other side of the stage to take another call before he rang up on the next act.

Josie had been on and was dressed for the street again, but I was still sitting on the edge of a trunk upstage, waiting to be called. It was now after five o'clock.

"Will you please go down there and ask that guy what time I go on?" I pleaded with her again.

She went to the first entrance, and came back with the message that an act from some musical comedy was to follow the troupe of Arab acrobats that had just finished, and that I'd most likely follow the musical comedy.

"How long does that run?" I inquired.

"I don't know. The stage manager's so busy, no one can find out a thing." Josie felt for me, all right, and I knew it, too, but my temper got the better of me and I said:

"This is a fine trick you played on me with your benefit stuff. These guys around here will think I'm some stage-struck amateur hanging around begging to go on."

"It isn't my fault, Georgie. Don't blame me." And she began to weep.

"You've certainly made a fine 'yap' out of me, that's what you've done," I added. This was more than she could stand, and she left the theater to start for home.

I sat there on the trunk until ten minutes of

six. I heard the audience cheering at the announcement of how much the gross receipts of the benefit had amounted to, and then the orchestra broke into "The Star-Spangled Banner" and the drop curtain came down as they banged into a Sousa march to play the audience out. I had been in the theater, dressed and ready to go on, for five hours and a half, and there I was sitting on the edge of a trunk up near the rear wall, still waiting to be called, when the performance was over.

All the actors and actresses, stars and near-stars, circus performers, and variety headliners, who had filled the entrances to watch the different acts as they went on and off now started toward the stage door, laughing, chatting, and carrying on all kinds of small talk as they passed me by without even a glance in my direction.

"Lucky lot of stiffs," I mumbled to myself. "I'll get even with all you birds some day. See if I don't."

I went to the dressing room and started to change my clothes. While I was "washing up" an old gentleman came in the room and said: "Too bad you didn't get on, kid. I guess they had too much show, eh?"

"Oh, I'm satisfied," I retorted as I threw the cold water in my eyes to wash away the tears. "I've got this guy's number, all right. They'll never get me for any more of their benefit bills. I'm through, but I'll get even with this guy Krauss. See if I don't."

"Did Krauss ask you to play the benefit?" inquired the old gentleman.

"Ask me to play it?" I sneered. "He sent forty messages to me through my sister. He just begged me to play it, that's all."

A few minutes later, on the way to the street, I passed the old gentleman in the hall. He was talking and giggling with two or three other men, and as I walked by they fairly screamed with laughter.

I found out later that the old gentleman was the manager of the Imperial, Mr. Krauss, himself.

CHAPTER XV

MY FIRST PUBLISHER

AFTER my "Imperial" benefit experience, I received no further offers for personal appearances the balance of the winter. Josie kept on with her single dancing act, and years afterward I learned through Joseph Vion, who became an agent, that he had endeavored time and again to induce mother and dad to accept engagements for their "double sketches," but, rather than have me discover that I was the only one of the quartette not wanted, they refused all offers and never mentioned the matter to me at all.

My state of mind during those months of idleness I wouldn't attempt to describe. I was absolutely certain that "dirty work" was being done by my enemies (probably the stage hands at the Union Square Theater) and the whole scheme was to keep me off the stage and break my spirit if possible, before I got the chance of exploiting my marvelous talents.

Day after day I'd go about mumbling to myself: "I'll show them yet. I'll have all these sour-grape birds bowing and scraping to me before long. . . . I'll make this whole theatrical business sit up and holler for help, that's what I'll do. I'll have my name posted and plastered up and down Broadway until I'm as well known as Hood's sarsaparilla. The first million dollars I get my hands on, I'll use it to buy that Koster and Bial dump and I'll take those two guys' names down and put my own up. Yes, and I'll get even with that guy Krauss, too; and as for Keith and Albee, well—they'll all hear from me. Every one of them."

This was a sample of the silent monologues I delivered as I walked about town, reading the sidewalks and dreaming my dreams of future fame and vengeance. From one music-publishing house to another I traipsed with my song manuscripts week in and week out. I had about exhausted the entire tin-pan-alley circuit. They all said the same thing.

"No market for songs of that kind."

"I'll write any kind you want," I'd reply.

"We don't want any right now," they'd answer.

"I'll get even with these guys," I'd mutter to myself as I'd roll up my manuscripts and take it on the run.

There was one concern, however, that I'd never had courage enough to visit. It was the establishment of M. Witmark & Sons. They were the big song publishers in those days. They still are, as far as I am concerned. I figured it would be useless to try for a hearing with that house, as they seemed to have first call on the output of every leading composer and lyric writer in the country. They'd be far too busy to bother with a new man; besides, I had them tabbed for a lot of swelled-headed guys, anyway.

"The big stiffs," I'd say to myself as I'd pass by their place. "Just goes to show how smart those babies in there are, publishing all that bum material written by a lot of 'hams,' and here I am, the best song writer in America, walking right by their door with four or five great big sure-fire hits under my arm."

One day out of sheer desperation, as I was about to pass their front door, I took a running start up the steps leading to the main entrance, and before I knew it I was inside, presenting my card to the young-lady attendant. She very courteously invited me to be seated and wait until Mr. Isidore was free. Mr. Isidore, by the way, turned out to be the eldest of the family of Witmark boys who were in business with their father. The young-lady attendant disappeared through a doorway in the rear, and a few minutes later returned, followed by an elderly man to whom she turned and spoke as she indicated me. "There's young Mr. Cohan sitting over there," she said.

The old gentleman came forward and extended his hand as I rose to greet him. It was the heartiest handshake I had received since I'd been in New York.

"Are you Jerry Cohan's son?" he asked.

"Yes, sir," I replied.

"Glad to meet you, mighty glad to meet you," he repeated. "I saw your father years ago in a play called 'The Molly Maguires,' down at Niblo's Garden."

"You don't say!" He had said it, of course, but I was trying to find words.

"I'm Mr. Witmark," he told me, as he gave my hand another shake.

He made me feel so welcome and so perfectly at ease that my heart (which had been up in my throat at the thought of having dared to approach this firm with my songs) slipped back in its regular place.

"Great pleasure to know you, Mr. Witmark," I said as I started to unroll my manuscripts.

"Come right with me, Georgie." He called me "Georgie." I knew then I was "in soft." "My son Isidore will see you right away." And as he said this he led me through a railing (the kind they have in police stations) to a door in the rear, then down an outer hall and into a private office.

A tall, dark-complexioned, well-groomed young man, wearing the thickest eyeglasses I'd ever seen, stood behind the busiest desk I'd ever looked at as we walked into the room. This same young man turned out to be the Mr. Isidore I'd heard everybody talking about in the front office.

"This is my son Issy," said Mr. Witmark, senior, and then he presented me to Issy. "This is Jerry Cohan's son Georgie."

"Glad to know you, young man," said Issy.

"Glad to know you, too," and we shook hands.

The old gentleman then went on to explain who I was and how much he had enjoyed my dad's performances years before. He hadn't stopped to inquire what I was there for, but was certainly advertising the fact that he wanted me to get a hearing.

"Give this boy every attention, Issy," he said as he shook hands with me again before leaving the room.

"You bet I will," returned young Witmark. And when the old gentleman had gone I sat down near the big desk and explained that I was there for the sole purpose of adding a few new hits to their catalogue.

"Let's hear what you've got," said young Witmark.

I moved to the piano and played and sang over several of my favorite ditties, and when I'd finished he rose from his chair behind the desk without any comment whatsoever, and said, "Pardon me just a moment." He went through a side door which I later found out was a gateway to the front office.

I naturally supposed that he had gone to get his entire family of brothers and partners to come and hear my masterpieces of composition. "We can't afford to let this kid get away from us; he's a genius." I could almost hear him whispering this to the gang out front.

It was fully five minutes before he returned, and when he did he said, in a very matter-of-fact way: "Now listen, young man. I've just had a talk with my father, and he seems very anxious to encourage you and help you in every possible way; but, to be truthful, there's only one of your songs that sounds like anything worth while to me. I mean that ballad you just sang."

"Do you refer to 'Why Did Nellie Leave Her Home?' " I asked.

"That's the one. Mind you, I'm not saying it's a good song," he went on. "As a matter of fact, it's a pretty bad song as it stands, but if you care to leave the manuscript here I'll see what can be done with it, and the chances are we'll be able to put it in some kind of shape and get it out and give you a start."

I didn't quite understand what he was getting at, but the thought struck me that he was trying to take advantage of my lack of business ability.

"This fellow knows in his heart that he's just heard four or five of the greatest songs ever written in any part of the world," I thought to myself. In a flash I was absolutely on to the fact that he was afraid I would demand big advance royalties, and so was using these methods to discourage and browbeat me into accepting whatever he cared to offer.

"What about the contract?" I inquired. He smiled at this. His work was great, all right, but I was eying him very closely.

"We'll talk about the contract later on, son, if you don't mind. I'm pretty busy right now." (I'd been there over an hour.) "Just leave your 'script on the piano over there and stroll in the latter part of next week, and I'll let you know definitely whether we can do anything about it or not."

I was on the verge of laughing down such an outrageous arrangement, when it suddenly occurred to me that, never having had a song published, it would at least be a step forward to a real hearing, so took the wild chance of leaving my manuscript and of being robbed and cheated. I merely said:

"All right, Mr. Witmark, whatever you say." His desk telephone rang and he said something about its being a "private matter," so I stepped out of his office without saying anything more.

On the way out, the old gentleman stopped me to shake hands again.

"Issy tells me you're trying to become a song writer," he chuckled. What did he mean, "trying to become a song writer?" How dared he patronize me in such a manner?

"Oh, yes," I answered, as indifferently as I could. "Anything to keep the pot boiling." He walked with me to the front door.

"Remember me to your father," he said as I started down the steps.

"I sure will, yes, sir," and I headed for Broadway.

"They're a gang of pirates and highwaymen in that place," I said to myself as I hurried along. I called the Witmarks everything villainous I could lay my tonguc to.

The fact that I'd actually "landed a song" finally loomed up before me. I was at last going to see my name as author and composer printed on the title page of a musical composition which would more than likely sell millions of copies. I instantly calmed down at the thought, and started whistling the refrain of "Why Did Nellie Leave Her Home?" and kept at it from Twenty-eighth Street all the way down Broadway to Union Square. When I arrived there I stopped to mingle with a group of song writers, to whom I began singing the praises of M. Witmark & Sons, and followed it up with a verse and chorus of the "Nellie" song.

When I had finished my rendition of this sad but beautiful ballad, a parody writer who was known as "McCann, the Song Factory," and who was a great favorite with the variety actors on account of his exceptional wit and ready remarks, said to me:

"Did you sell that song to the Witmarks?"

"Sure. They grabbed it the minute I pulled it on them."

"Put it there, kid," and he grabbed my hand. "You're the best business man I ever met."

"What do you mean by that?" I asked.

The gang started backing away from the curb, to get more laughing space.

"Have you ever heard the song yourself?" went on McCann.

"Ever heard it? Certainly? Didn't I just tell you that I wrote it?"

"I know you wrote it, but have you ever heard it?"

"Certainly, I've heard it. Didn't I just sing it?"

"I know you sang it, but I'm asking you again, have you ever heard it?" he insisted.

By this time the rest of the crowd that had moved away were fairly convulsed, falling over one another, trying to see who could laugh the loudest. It took me till then to realize that I was being "kidded" by McCann.

"You'll get rich shoe stumping me."

"We'll never be rich enough," he replied, "to repay you for writing a song like that. You deserve a monument over in Calvary."

Another wild outburst sent me on my way down Fourteenth Street and to the boarding house, where I imparted the news to my family that the Witmarks were moving heaven and earth in their efforts to get my name to a long-term contract. I had all the publishers in town fighting for my future compositions and had just closed a big deal for "Why Did Nellie Leave Her Home?"

"Hurray for you, son!" shouted Dad.

Josie threw her arms about my neck and kissed me.

Mother wept with joy.

"I told you I'd fold this town up and put it in my pocket, didn't I? Well, you just watch me from now on."

The supper bell rang and "America's best song writer" spent the following half hour complaining bitterly about the boarding-house food.

CHAPTER XVI

GETTING BUSY

DURING the two or three weeks that followed, I devoted most of my spare time to "buttonholing" acquaintances, edging my way into groups, and annoying people generally by advertising the fact, with words and music, that "Nellie had left her home." I carried the royalty contract, which Witmark had given me, in my coat pocket, and proudly displayed it every chance I got.

I sang the song at least thirty times a day. No one escaped me. Acrobats, magicians, jugglers, monologuists, wire walkers, in fact all of Union Square, listened most patiently as I moved about here and there, rendering the brilliant ballad to them all.

When the advance professional copies of the song came out, much to my astonishment and chagrin, I discovered that an entirely new set of lyrics had been written to fit my melody. The only thing left of the original set of words was the title line. My indignation knew no bounds.

"They can't do this to me," I declared to myself over and over again as I read and reread the new version of my brain child. "I'll sue them, that's what I'll do. I'll put them in jail for this."

And then the terrible, humiliating thought struck me.

"Here I've been singing the song as I wrote it for weeks and weeks to everybody I know. Now they'll hear this distortion and naturally guess that the whole thing has been revised. I'll be laughed at for allowing my name to be signed to a lyric that some one else has written." My blood boiled with anger. How dared they do such a thing without first consulting me? "They've ruined my beautiful song," I thought.

With fire in my eyes and murder in my heart, I started to tear up Fourteenth Street on a dead run for the Witmark offices. As I flew by the Union Square Hotel at Fifteenth Street, a familiar voice called to me.

"Hey there, kid! What's your hurry? Is the sheriff after you?"

I turned and recognized McCann, the parody writer who had kidded me so unmercifully about the song a few weeks before. An idea struck me. A new twist on the thing came in a flash. I quit running and turned back to speak to him.

"Hello! How are you, Mac? Glad to see you." I shook hands with him as I pulled up, puffing like a locomotive. In my heart I was sore on this fellow, but there was a method in my madness of the moment.

"Remember that song I sang to you a short time ago?" I asked, in a friendly way.

"Remember it? I'll never forget it. I've been whistling it ever since. Wait now. I'll get it in a second." He started studying the sky to find the tune.

"That's funny. It's slipped my mind this second," he finally said. "Just start it for me. Go on, hum it once, will you?"

I was looking for something like this, but I held my temper.

"I've rewritten the whole thing," I said. "Would you mind listening to it?"

"You mean you'll sing it for nothing? No charge of any kind?" he eluded.

"Oh, quit stringing, will you, Mac? I want your opinion."

"All right," he said, "but just sing it—just the words and music without any gestures. The motions take my mind off the story."

I took this joke request good-naturedly, whipped out the professional copy, and spread it open.

"Oh, you've had it published, eh?" He seemed surprised to see the printed sheet.

"Sure. Just out. I've done a lot of work on it, though, since you heard it. See if you think I've helped it any." And I began to sing the new version.

He appeared to become interested as I sang along. When I'd finished, he said:

"Say, kid, did you write that set of words or did your father write 'em? On the level, tell me the truth."

"Do you suppose I'd put my name on it if my father had written it?" And I pointed to the credit line under the title, "Words and music by George M. Cohan."

"Well, I've got to hand it to you, that's a real song now." His manner had changed entirely. "The other lyric you had was terrible! On the square, it was awful!"

"That was just the first draft," I explained. "Think I've helped it, eh?"

"Helped it?" and he burst into a laugh. "Listen, kid," he went on, "I'm going to tell you a secret. I thought you were a 'hick,' but I want to say right now that anyone who can turn a comic song into a ballad is a smart guy. That thing sounds like a hit to me."

"It does, on the square?" I was half "sore" and half delighted.

"Yes, sir, you've got a good song there." He was sincere now, I could tell. "How far uptown are you going?" he asked, and we started to move.

"To Thirty-fourth," I stalled. I wasn't going anywhere in particular just then. I had decided to stay away from Witmarks for a while.

"I'll keep you company as far as Twenty-third," he said as we strolled along. It was the first time any one of the Union Square crowd had voluntarily "joined out" with me, and I was proud as a peacock to think that I was receiving proper recognition at last.

I spent the next few days running around and singing the new version of "Nellie" to those who had heard the original, explaining that I had revised the thing completely. They all agreed that I had made it into an infinitely better song.

Little by little I came to realize that the new lyric was much more singable than mine. The sort of jingle that only an experienced and expert "word writer" could have done. I didn't admit this to the publishers, however. As a matter of fact, I never went near their offices. I didn't even acknowledge receipt of the advance copies they'd sent. I was too ashamed.

Over twenty years went by before I ever laid eyes on any of the Witmarks again, and when that time came it was my turn to do a little rewriting and revising. We'll come to that later on.

I have never learned to this day whether that first published song of mine was ever sung in public, or if a single copy ever actually sold, but I do know that my name as author and composer appearing on a title page gave me a certain standing with song writers and publishers. I became one of the regular "hangers-on" around several music houses, and was observing and alert enough to keep my eyes open and my ears cocked. My heart was set on being a popular-song writer. I practiced verse writing night and day.

"The words must jingle, the words must jingle," I'd keep repeating over and over again.

I could play four chords on the piano in F sharp. I'd vamp these four chords and hum tunes to myself for hours at a time. I never got any further than the four F sharp chords, by the way. I've used them ever since.

Inside of six months, during which I worked like a trojan to improve my style of melody and learn how to jingle words in rhyme, no less than half a dozen manuscripts of mine had been accepted for publication.

I played no favorites with the publishers. I'd sell a song wherever I could get the price. The price was from ten to twenty-five dollars, according to the subject and merits of the thing. The paying of so much a copy as royalties was an exceptional arrangement in those days. The average song writer (comparatively few at the time) was usually pressed for ready cash, and couldn't afford to gamble.

One of the songs I turned out that winter was a little fanciful ballad called "Venus, My Shining Love." I sold it for twenty-five dollars. Later on, when the song started to sell, the publisher made me a present of two hundred and fifty.

"You might write a better song than that some day," he remarked as he handed me the check. "But to tell you the truth, young fellow, I doubt it."

That was thirty years ago, and I know now what a good guess the publisher made. It's still the best song I ever wrote.

At this stage of the game I became a pretty busy kid. Besides turning out one or two songs a week for publication, I scribbled parodies and patter for comedians, comic songs and extra verses for serio comics, and even took a shot at a couple of afterpieces for burlesque shows. After a while, I got to writing sketches for variety teams, and orders came in so fast that I found it impossible to supply the demand. With parodies in every pocket and sketch manuscripts under my arm, I was soon the envy of all the pencil pushers in the variety branch of the theatrical game.

Finally, Lew Dockstader, who was the leading monologist of the day, engaged me to turn out the material for his new act, and my self-importance began to assert itself. I walked about town with all the airs and manners of a very superior person.

One rainy night, when the New York streets were more or less deserted, I trudged through the storm, juggling around in my mind the plot of a comedy sketch I was preparing. I couldn't concentrate unless I walked. I can't yet, for that matter.

Suddenly I looked up and discovered myself standing in front of the darkened auditorium of Keith's Union Square Theater. I smiled to myself.

"I wonder what all those 'wise-cracking' stage hands in there think now?" I thought. "When they see these sketches of mine, and hear my name announced as the author and composer of all these songs? I've certainly made those guys ashamed of themselves, all right."

Another chuckle of satisfaction, and I went back to my comedy plot and walked on in the direction of the boarding house. As I passed the German Savings Bank at the corner of Fourteenth Street and Fourth Avenue, where I had eleven hundred dollars deposited in my own name, my thoughts switched back to the Keith stage hands, and I murmured to myself, "Union Square is mine, *now for Broadway*."

CHAPTER XVII

BACK TO THE PLATFORM

A FEW weeks later, out of a clear sky, Josie said to me, "Georgie, I don't think we're managing ourselves very well, and it's up to you and me to have a chat with mother and dad and decide just what our future is going to be."

"What do you mean, sis?" I didn't quite follow her.

"Well, this is all very well," she continued, "this business of my doing the single dancing act (she by now had made an exceptional success and was in demand and playing every week), and the headway you've made with your songs and sketches has made us all very happy, but we've got to look to the future and make up our minds pretty soon whether we're going to stick together or not."

I asked her to be a little more explicit, so she continued:

"Well, I think we should make a stand right now, that unless these managers agree to accept the four act, we'll quit the variety business altogether and get dad to put out the road show again."

This was an amazing stand for her to take, and about as unselfish a thought as a person could have. Here was this little girl, who had scored a big personal hit in New York's leading music halls, willing to make the big sacrifice of "going back to the sticks" in order to keep the family together. However, it was just like Josie. There never was anyone just like Josie.

I was anxious to get back behind the footlights, so naturally the suggestion appealed to me immediately. All the song and sketch writing in the world could never make me forget that I was a "trouper" first, last, and always, and in my heart of hearts I'd been hoping that something might happen to put me back in my dancing shoes. I never dreamed, though, that Josie would ever be satisfied to throw aside the reputation she had made as a "single turn."

That afternoon the four of us talked the matter over, and Josie was so insistent and so convincing with her argument, we finally decided that from that time on it was to be the

Four Cohans or no Cohans at all, and dad sent word to all the agencies to that effect. The following Saturday night Josie terminated her New York engagements and we sent an "ad" to the *Clipper* announcing the reunion of the Four.

There wasn't any wild scramble on the part of the variety managers to book the act, however, as they still wanted Josie alone. The best we could do was to book a week at Zipp's Casino in Brooklyn.

Zipp's was nothing more than an old-fashioned beer hall that charged admission and offered four or five specialty turns to entertain the "lager" drinkers. We accepted this engagement with the hope that Hyde and Behman, the big Brooklyn managers, would drop in to see the act and engage us for their Adams Street Theater. It was the ambition of every variety act in those days to play Hyde and Behman's Adams Street Theater.

In reply to a letter sent to them, asking if they would be kind enough to look us over with a view to future bookings, we received the following:

THE FOUR COHANS
DEAR SIRS:
Your act would not interest us. We note that you are appearing at Zipp's Casino.
Respectfully yours,
HYDE AND BEHMAN.

We didn't learn until then that the Hyde and Behman management had a set rule never to play an act that had appeared at any other Brooklyn variety house. We were broken-hearted when we discovered this fact. We had foolishly, but innocently, made the mistake. It didn't turn out to be a fatal mistake, however, as you will learn later on.

During the week at Zipp's, old George Huber, the manager, who had heard about the letter we had received from Hyde and Behman, came to us and said: "I want you folks to understand that this house is open to you any week you happen to have open. Stay here next week if you care to, and the week after, too, if you like; stay here as long as you please; but whatever you do, don't go around worrying about Hyde and Behman. There's one house in Brooklyn the Four Cohans can always play and you can tell Hyde and Behman I said so." This

A SCENE FROM "THE LITTLE MILLIONAIRE"

COHAN IN THE RÔLE OF HIS OWN FATHER'S SON

attitude of Huber healed the wound to some extent, and we took advantage of his offer and played there five or six weeks.

The only other booking we received was for a single week's engagement in New Haven, where S. Z. Poli had just opened his first variety theater.

We realized that there was little or no chance for us in the East, but we were bent on sticking to our guns and the "four act," so we jumped to the Middle West and played the Moore Circuit of Museums. We accepted a third of the salary, for the Four doing five shows a day, that Josie had been receiving for eight performances a week as a single turn. It seemed an unbusiness-like thing to do, but we all felt that it would turn out for the best, and, anyway, it kept us together, like the proverbial Brown's cows.

We hopped-scotched about, playing the honky-tonks for several months after that, and with five and six shows a day (Sunday included), along with grinding out songs and sketches at nights into the wee hours of the mornings, it kept me whirling about a bit, as busy as a buzz saw.

I was earning pretty big money for a kid my

age, turning out this stage material, so from the financial standpoint we were doing fairly well. The thing that made me happiest of all, however, was the fact that I was back on the stage again. A round of applause from even a dime-museum audience meant far more to me than a fat certified check from a song publisher or sketch team. Though only sixteen years of age, I was already a "dyed-in-the-wool" song-and-dance man. I still am, for that matter—always will be, I dare say.

When the theatrical season came to an end, we jumped back East to spend the summer at North Brookfield, Massachusetts, a little town about fifty miles from Boston, where my grandmother lived.

We stopped over in New York for the purpose of letting the agents know that we were still on earth and "at liberty." We were hurriedly booked at the Central Music Hall, a variety theater in Sixty-seventh Street, the very day we arrived in town. They ran short of an act, and we happened in at the right moment.

The night we opened there, Gus Williams, the well-known German-dialect comedian, was in front and, after seeing our performance, came back stage and engaged us for the following season to support him in a play called "April Fool." Williams used to tour the country very successfully season after season, being what was known as a great "road star," and we were the happiest theatrical family on earth when dad signed the contract the next morning.

"You and I are going to get along all right, young man," Williams said to me while we were shaking hands back stage.

"I hope so, Mr. Williams," I replied.

"I think I can make an actor of you." He was sizing me up very carefully.

"Think you can, eh?" I didn't care so much for that crack.

"Well, at least I can try," he went on. "You've got a personality, and that gives me something to work on. Of course, it's a pretty big job for a kid like you. It's one of the best low-comedy parts ever written, and this fellow Midgely, who played it last season, made a sensational hit. The trouble will be that you'll have to repeat a lot of towns where he's been seen. He's a hard man to follow."

"I'll follow him all right," I assured him.

"That's the stuff," he approved; "that's the spirit that will win every time. I'll give you the full benefit of my experience and direction, and if you keep up your nerve you'll have better than an even chance to make it."

"Oh, don't worry about me. I'll make it all right." And then I muttered to myself, "This guy hates himself."

"I'll tell you one thing, kid," he said. "If you've half as much talent as you have confidence, you'll be a great actor some day." He laughed and shook hands, "Good-by." And that was the last I saw of him until the August rehearsals.

"That fellow's got a fat chance to tell me how to play that part." (I broke right into a monologue the minute his back was turned.) "Anybody would think, to hear him handing out his line of talk, that he was opening up a school of acting or something. He's going to direct me. Gee! That's pretty good. That's the laugh of the year with me. Best comedy ever written, eh? This bird Midgely was good, was he? Well, we'll see about that." (Business of whistling and trying to forget it; short pause; then another outburst.) "Can you beat that guy talking to me like that?" (A short, forced laugh.) "That's a hot one, that is. That would burn anybody's fingers." Williams didn't know what he was in for.

CHAPTER XVIII

FIRST MEETING WITH MY LAWYER

OFF we went to North Brookfield for our summer vacation (1895). Quite a town, too. It always looked to me as though a scenic artist had painted it on the side of a hill. Four thousand people in the burg, and most of them talked the kind of talk that Ring Lardner writes.

Not being able to interest myself in post-office conversations, I went into seclusion and started out to make a record as a sketch writer by pounding out one-act plays at the rate of not less than two a week.

"Why don't you quit grinding for a while, son, and get out and play a little baseball with the boys?" dad used to say.

"Yes, I wish you would, Georgie." This from mother.

"I'm busy to-day—I'll play to-morrow." But to-morrow never came.

Not that I didn't enjoy playing around as

much as other boys my age, but I was having so much fun with my work that the work seemed to me to be nothing but fun.

Writing lyrics, composing tunes, scheming and working out plots for one-act sketches, up and down the room, up and down the room, eight to ten hours a day. Pound, pound, pound. I was as serious about it all as though the great American theater absolutely depended on my output.

There was one young fellow in this town who took quite a fancy to me. His name was Dennis O'Brien. (It was whispered that his ancestors came from Ireland.) The kids all called him "Captain," a distinction he'd earned because of the "cocky" manner in which he led the march of the parochial pupils from the village church to the schoolhouse.

We were about the same age and he was the only person around who seemed at all interested in the fact that I was a "worker." I used to bring my manuscripts to his house for spelling corrections and instruction in grammar.

"I often wonder what these people think when they read your sketches," he chuckled, one night.

"You put every word on paper exactly the way it's pronounced, don't you?"

"Oh, don't worry about that," I replied. "Most of the guys I write for can't read, anyway."

We used to have long talks about our respective futures.

"Are you going to stay in this town all your life?" I asked, during one of these chats.

"No siree, I'm going to New York City and be a lawyer," he announced.

"Maybe you'll be my lawyer some day," I suggested.

"You never can tell," he replied.

And we'd sit on the front porch, dreaming of Shakespeare and Blackstone, until his mother would send me home and chase him to bed.

Fifteen years later, when he came to New York to practice law, I was the first client to walk into his office. He's been my councilor and business adviser ever since. Spelling corrections are still in order, by the way—Dennis F. O'Brien at the teacher's desk. But to get back to North Brookfield and the summer of 1895.

One of the songs I sent on to New York for

publication, during our stay there, was a coon ditty entitled, "Hot Tamale Alley." May Irwin had put it in her show, and had popularized it to such an extent that by the time we got back to New York in August it was one of the hits of the town.

"May Irwin's singing a song of mine," I thought. "I wonder what those Witmark guys think now." If the Queen of England had kissed me, my chest couldn't have expanded any more.

On the way to the "April Fool" rehearsal I had a quiet laugh all to myself. I raved on, "I'll make this bird Williams understand that I'm no 'ham.' He'll forget any one else ever played the part when I get a crack at it."

We were called for the first reading of the play the day we arrived in town. The company assembled in a little rehearsal hall on Third Avenue.

Mr. Williams, after greeting the supporting cast in star-like fashion, spread the manuscript open on a table, asked us all to pull up chairs, and we sat around and listened while he read the dialogue and explained the bits of business and byplay and pointed out and went through the mechanics of each scene as carefully as he could.

When he had finished (it took several hours to read the thing) he turned to me and said, "Well, young man, that's a great part you've got. Don't you think so?"

The entire company, my family included, looked in my direction. Josie started coughing; she felt that something was coming. All during the reading of the play I had been shaking my head and telegraphing the fact that I was bored to death.

"I think it's the makings of a good part," I answered, "if you'll let me fix it up a little."

Josie coughed again. Father fumbled with his watch chain. Mother started taking off and putting on her ring, a sure sign of nervousness on mother's part. The balance of the cast sat staring at me in amazement.

"Fix it up a little? What do you mean?" And Williams leaned on the table. He didn't quite "get me."

"Well, I mean I think I can help it a whole lot."

"Help the part, you mean?"

"Sure. Help the whole play if you'll let me

fool around with the 'script for a day or two."

He pushed his chair away from the table and stood up.

"Say, who in hell do you think you are?" He blurted this, and then, turning quickly to the female members of the company, said, "Pardon me, ladies"; then to me again, "Are you trying to get a laugh, or are you just naturally fresh?"

"Well, there's nothing to get sore about, Mr. Williams." I knew I'd slipped. "I just want to be of whatever assistance I can. I'm perfectly willing to do the job for nothing."

"What job?" He all but shouted this.

I'd slipped again. I realized it, too, but I went on.

"Just to prove that it isn't a matter of money with me, if you'll postpone rehearsals for a few days and let me take a shot at that 'script, I'll turn it into a regular play free of charge. That's fair enough, isn't it?"

Williams turned to dad.

"Jerry, does this kid of yours think he's a comedian, or is he just a plain everyday crackpot?" This created a general laugh.

Dad tried to laugh it off, too. "Oh, Georgie's all right, Gus. He's just a boy with big ideas about himself, that's all." And then to me, "That's a wonderful part Mr. Williams has handed you, and if you're smart enough to listen and take advantage of his direction it'll be the chance of your life." Then to Williams, "It's a great chance for all of us, Gus, and we want you to know that we appreciate it, too."

"I know, but what's the idea of this kid making a crack like that?" He refused to dismiss the thing.

"Will you do me a favor and forget it, Gus?" urged dad.

"All right, we'll let it go, but——" and Williams walked over to where I was standing and shook his cigar at my nose. "You save all your comedy remarks for the sidewalk after this. I've never stood for a fresh kid in any of my companies yet, and I'm not going to begin now. Do you get that?"

"I didn't mean to be fresh, Mr. Williams."

"Well, you were, and see that it doesn't happen again. Is that settled."

"Yes, sir."

And he clapped his hands and shouted, "Everybody back here at two-thirty for the first act." We were dismissed for lunch.

On the way to the boarding house dad went after me hammer and tongs.

"You've got to cut this stuff out. Do you understand? I'm just about losing all patience with you. Don't you realize that you insulted that man by belittling his play? What's getting into you, anyway? Where do you suppose this thing is going to end?" A short pause—and he continued: "Haven't you any consideration whatever for your mother and sister and me? For the love of Heaven, come down to earth, please. If you don't, something's going to happen, you mark my words."

Mother and Josie walked along without uttering a word.

"Well, I was only trying to help," I argued

"Yes, you helped a lot, you did. Very nearly helped us out of a job." And he increased his gait to get ahead of me. I hurried and caught up with him.

"I'm sorry, dad." I meant it, too.

"Well, I hope you are, and I hope this will teach you a lesson to keep your mouth closed after this."

Nothing more was said for several blocks. I finally tugged at dad's arm to get his attention.

"Listen, dad," I began. "Will you do me a favor?"

"What is it you want?"

"Will you answer me truthfully if I ask you something?"

"Of course I will."

"Well, on the square now, between you and me, don't you really think I could fix up that play if he'd let me take a crack at it?"

Josie heard this and answered: "Don't be silly, Georgie. The play's been a big success for two years already."

"I wouldn't care if it had been a success for twenty years. I still think it's a bum piece and I know I could fix it up."

"Georgie, please, please!" mother pleaded.

Nothing more was said until we got to the boarding house. We entered through the basement door as a short cut to the dining room, and when we got inside, the strains of "Hot Tamale Alley" came floating from the parlor on the floor above. A sister team was rehearsing the ditty with a view of placing it in their act.

"I guess a few songs like that wouldn't help that play any, eh?" I remarked as we sat at the table.

I won't attempt a description of any of the boarders in this Fourteenth Street establishment. Suffice it to say that they were all as hungry as they looked, and always on hand for the mad dash every time the dining-room bell rang. They were there full strength when we arrived for lunch.

A song-and-dance man sitting next to me said, "I hear you folks are going with 'April Fool'? Is that right?"

"Yes. We just came from rehearsal."

"What part are you playing?"

"The low comedy."

"Not the part Midgely played last season?"

"Yes. Why?"

"Well, you've got a fine young job in front of you." And he laughed so heartily that his napkin slipped out from under his collar.

"What's the idea of the outburst?" I inquired. He tried to answer, but couldn't, he was laughing so hard.

"Was Midgely a big hit?" I asked.

"A big hit? He was a riot." He tucked the napkin again and went after the apple sauce.

"Fried sausage or baked beans?" the waitress

leaned over and asked as she brushed away the crumbs in front of me.

"Neither; just bring me a cup of coffee." My appetite had entirely disappeared. The song-and-dance man had killed all desire for food.

I swallowed the coffee, ran upstairs to my room, and stood in front of the bureau looking glass, where I talked to Gus Williams like a "Dutch uncle" until Josie called to me that the folks were ready, and we all started back to rehearsal.

CHAPTER XIX

THE CRITICS AT WORK

THEN followed three weeks of rehearsals with the "April Fool" piece, during which I stood the "gaff" without a murmur. Williams spent most of his time rehearsing me in the scenes I played opposite him.

"Midgely used to do so and so," and "Midgely scored a laugh by such and such a bit of business," he'd explain during the direction.

"If this guy thinks I'm going to give an imitation of this other bird, he's crazy. I've got my own conception of this thing, but I'll let him have his own way about it till the opening night." Those were my feelings in the matter, but, without expressing them, continued to follow his instructions to the letter, so everything went along swimmingly for the time being.

We opened the season in Newark the first week in September, and I walked on the stage at the first performance and offered an entirely different idea of the part than either Williams or Midgely had ever thought of. Instead of the "silly kid" character I was supposed to be and had been rehearsed to play, I twisted the thing around to a flip, impudent, dashing young juvenile in a low-comedy make-up. When the first act curtain fell, Williams rushed at me.

"What are you trying to do, ruin this play? What's the matter with you, anyway?"

"What's the matter with you?" I came back. "I made them laugh, didn't I?" My family ran over to protect me. The rest of the cast gathered around, too.

"You go on there and play the next two acts the way you were rehearsed. Do you understand? If you don't, you'll go out of that stage door, with your trunk flying after you." Then turning to dad, who stood there white with rage, Williams continued, "Jerry, did you see what this kid did to me in that first act?"

For the first time in his life, dad took a swing at me. I ducked. Mother and Josie screamed with fright, and I took it on the run to the stage door and out to the alley. Josie came rushing after me.

"Come on, Georgie. You've got to dress for the second act. You don't want to hold this curtain." The poor kid was trembling like a leaf.

"Not a chance. I'm through with this troupe right now. That guy in there talking about ruining his play! Gee! that's rich, that is! If I couldn't write a better play than that blindfolded, with my left hand, I'd do a row of flips into the East River."

As I said this I parked myself on the tailboard of a transfer truck standing in the alley, and lit a cigarette. Josie came over to me and begged:

"Please, Georgie, please! The folks are in there, crying their eyes out. You can't quit in the middle of a performance."

At that moment Williams appeared at the stage door, his coat and vest off, his wig in his hand, and his collar loosened and dangling at his neck. He looked like a wild man to me as he rushed toward the truck, followed by mother, who was weeping, and dad with his arm about her, trying to console her, and the balance of the cast tagging on behind.

"Georgie said he'd finish the performance, Mr. Williams. Everything's all right," Josie announced, as they all came forward.

"What the hell are you doing out here?" Williams roared at me.

"Waiting for my trunk. You said you'd throw it out. Go ahead and do it." As I said this I slid up from the tailboard and climbed to the driver's seat. I was afraid to let him get near enough to take a punch at me.

"Get down from there and come in and finish this show," dad hollered, and started to hop on the truck to get at me.

"Wait a second, Jerry. Don't do that." As mother said this, she pulled him back.

"Yes, wait a minute, dad," I repeated as I stood on the front seat and raised my hand for silence. "I've got something to say to everybody here." I had spied the house policeman coming through the stage door, followed by the entire crew carrying stage braces and hurrying to what they evidently thought was going to be an alley fight. In a flash I realized that I was "in bad," and decided to work fast and square myself as soon as I could.

"I'm sorry this thing happened," I went on. "I apologize most abjectly" (I'd heard Williams use the word) "to you, dad, to mother, to Mr. Williams, and everybody here. What I did in that first act I did with all the good intentions in the world. I was only trying to help the play, that's all."

"This play doesn't need any help," shouted the company stage manager. He was a little wizened-up, bald-headed guy with gold teeth. I hated him, anyway.

"Maybe it doesn't," I shouted back at him, "but I thought it did. However, if you're all willing to forget what's happened, we'll call all bets off and I'll go back in there and play the part the way you want it, and promise never to open my mouth again for the rest of the season."

"Well, then, come on and get at it," hollered Williams, anxious to get the curtain up, and, without further comment, made a dash for the stage door, followed by the entire company, including myself. We rushed to our respective dressing rooms and "made up" for the second act.

The balance of the performance sailed along without any deaths being reported. The members of the company passed me up like a white check, however, so I began figuring to myself that a little more "squaring" would be necessary to stave off a riot at the finish of the play.

When the curtain fell on the grand musical finale, as the program called it, I walked up to Mr. Williams and added this to my earlier apology:

"Mr. Williams," I began, in the presence of the entire cast, "I want you to know that I'm heartily sorry for what I did in the first act to-night, and if you'll overlook it and ask these other folks to forgive me, I'll guarantee you'll have no further trouble from me as long as I'm in the company."

This seemed to make a hit with him, because he smiled and laid his hand on my shoulder, and said: "All right, Georgie, we'll overlook it this time; and if you'll behave yourself, we'll all promise not to mention it again." He turned to the company. "Did you hear that, ladies and gentlemen?" They all said they did and agreed to forgive and forget with a uniform nod of their heads.

"Thanks, Mr. Williams," I muttered, in hang-dog fashion. This sort of thing was very hard for me to take.

"The only thing I'm sorry about," Williams added, "is that these stage hands will more than likely imagine that you're a swelled-headed kid. Of course, we all know better, but you see——"

I interrupted him at this point. "There's nothing swelled-headed about me at all, Mr. Williams. I'm too smart to get that way. I could have had a swelled head a long time ago if I wanted to. Why, I've published over two hundred songs. Right now May Irwin is making the hit of her life with one of them. Look at all the sketches I've written for variety teams. I've got a dozen of 'em playing around the country at this minute. But I don't go round bragging about it. No, sir, there's nothing swelled headed about me. You didn't hear me making any wise cracks just because I happened to take four or five encores on my specialty in the second act to-night, did you? No, sir, I'm not that sort of a little guy, and I want all the members of this company and the stage hands and everybody else to understand it, too."

Williams stood there staring at me for several seconds, and then broke into a hearty laugh. The balance of the troupe followed suit. They all started toward the dressing rooms, leaving me in the center of the last-act set with the bald-headed "gold-toothed" stage manager, who stood with his hands on his hips, looking at me as though I were a freak. After a couple of seconds he turned and shouted to the departing cast, "Rehearsal, ten-thirty to-morrow morning." Then he swung around to me again, "Come on," he said, and half pushed me aside. "Give us the stage, please." And he clapped his hands and hollered, "Strike," and the crew got busy removing the scenery.

I started to walk to my dressing room, and as I look back now I'll swear it seemed the longest walk I'd ever taken in all my life.

I intended to stop in my parents' room before I retired that night, and explain to them again how much I regretted my mistake, but on passing their door, which happened to be half opened, I heard dad say:

"Of course, I don't want to break the boy's spirit, or anything like that, but just one more exhibition of this kind and he's going to get all that's coming to him, and believe me, it won't be conversational punishment, either."

On hearing this I quietly sneaked to my own room and started to write a poem called "The Best Dad in the World." The first two lines ran—

My father gave me everything that any father could.
He never laid a hand on me; I knew he never would.

My poetry was always written to fit the situation.

The following morning the Newark dramatic critic, after giving the piece a fairly good notice, spoke of me as follows:

> The fourth member of the Cohan family was programed as George M. What the "M" stands for was not revealed last evening. It was, however, the only one thing about his performance that reminded us at all of Midgely who appeared here in the same part last season.

"I wonder what that guy means by that?" I said to myself, as I read it over the second time.

No one referred to the notice at rehearsal that morning, and, although I kept on wondering whether it was a "knock" or a "boost," I was far too proud to bring the matter up, so I let it go by default until that evening when the gold-toothed stage manager came into my dressing room to hang up his coat.

"The morning paper kind of 'panned' you a little, didn't it?" he remarked. He was glad of it, too. I got it all in a flash.

"Sure it did," I shot back. "And I'll bet you or anybody else a hundred-dollar note that the guy that wrote that notice has got a lot of gold stuck in his teeth."

He gave me a hard look, removed his coat from the hook, and walked out of the room. You can imagine what that baby thought of me the balance of the season.

CHAPTER XX

ACCIDENTS WILL HAPPEN

FOR thirty-five of the longest weeks of my life we toured throughout the country with "April Fool," and wherever we played, the set speech seemed to be, "What became of the fellow that played your part last season?" I listened to the singing of his praises from Belfast, Maine, to Kansas City.

Even then, as a seventeen-year-old trouper, I solemnly swore to myself that never again, if I could possibly side-step the issue, would I follow any man in a part he had created.

I lived up to this promise for twenty-five years. In 1918, however, I was forced into another man's rôle in a comedy which I had written for the Cohan Theater. But this time the laugh was not on me. The other fellow hopped out because he thought the play was a failure, and I jumped in to prove that it wasn't. I managed to save the situation by turning the piece into a genuine box-office success.

I'd like to whisper a word to the reader right here.

"If at times I appear to be 'boosting' myself a little too much, I wish you would call my attention to the fact, because I wouldn't have you get the wrong idea of me for the world."

"Oh, that's all right," says the reader. "No apologies necessary."

"All right. If you feel that way about it, I'll go straight along."

When Gus Williams handed us our two weeks' notice in Chillicothe, Ohio (which was the outcome of a scrap I had with the gold-toothed stage manager), he spied me standing in front of the local opera house and came over to me and said, "I want to thank you, young fellow, for a very pleasant season."

"What kind of a speech is that?" I pretended not to "get" him, but I understood all right.

"Listen to me, Georgie," he went on. "If ever you're lucky enough to have your own show, take my tip and never have anybody but full-grown men in the cast."

"Now look here, Mr. Williams, you've got

me all wrong." He tried to get away, but I followed him down the street. "I don't mean to be fresh," I argued. "I'll admit that I'm a little overbearing once in a while, but you've got to consider that I've had a great deal on my mind besides this part I've been playing. I've been sitting up night after night writing sketches and songs all season long. You people don't understand me at all. I'm a busy little guy, I am; my mind is working every minute. I try hard enough not to fly off the handle. I want to be pleasant and congenial like the average person, but my nerves are shot to pieces all the time. Letters and telegrams every hour in the day for a song here or a sketch there, and checks and money orders to take care of, all the correspondence to clean up and a thousand other things to do. You know this salary you've been paying us means nothing in my life at all. Why, I earn more money in a day than you pay us in a week. You see, you ought to take all these things into consideration, and so should all the other people in the company, too. You know darned well I haven't got a swelled head. You know I'm too smart to get like that, but I've been under a great strain since I've been with this show."

"So have I; so has everybody else in the company," he went on. "There's one thing I'll say for you, Georgie; you've convinced me that capital punishment is an absolute necessity."

By this time we'd reached the hotel, and he walked into the office and to the desk and asked for his key. Then he started for the elevator. I followed him.

"Will you listen to me for just a minute, please?" I said.

"I've been listening to you all season," he answered as he shook the key in my face, "and if you get into this elevator with me, so help me God, I'll grab the lever and run it right through the roof."

That was the last time he spoke to me until fifteen years later when we met in the lobby of the Knickerbocker Hotel in New York, where we played the scene all over again, much to the amusement of several friends of his, to whom he had introduced me.

When we closed with "April Fool" we were booked for a single week's engagement in Buffalo, on account of being old stock favorites in the town. This time it was at the Court Street Theater.

At the Monday-morning music rehearsal a strange thing happened. A thing that, although purely accidental, eventually turned out to be the reason for my subsequent success as an eccentric dancer.

I had always done a dance in the four act, to the tune of "Coming Through the Rye." It was an old-fashioned "essence of old Virginia" dance. It had never taken especially well with the audiences, but was necessary to the act in order to give Josie a chance to make a change of costume.

I'd always claimed that the dance was all right, but that the music killed it, so I asked the orchestra leader that morning if he could substitute some other tune for "Coming Through the Rye."

"What kind of a dance is it?" he asked.

"An old-fashioned essence," I replied.

"I've got just the thing, but it's at home. I'll bring it around for the matinée."

"That'll be fine," I said, and let it go at that.

When we got to the spot in the act for the dance at the matinée that afternoon, I gave the leader the cue, and the orchestra started up the music (the new arrangement he had brought from his home). It was the weirdest melody I had ever heard, and the drummer accompanied the tune with a tomtom effect, characteristic of the American Indian. I tried my best to get into the dance, but my sense of rhythm was keen enough to make me immediately realize that the thing broke time, and also that the piece did not carry an even number of bars. The melody continued, but instead of dancing I stood dead still in the center of the stage, trying to figure out just why I couldn't do my essence steps to the music. It suddenly dawned on me that, instead of its being in six-eight time, to which I'd always done this particular dance, the thing they were playing was in two-four time.

Under ordinary circumstances, I should probably have stopped the orchestra and requested "Coming Through the Rye," but there were several theatrical friends of ours out front that afternoon, among them being Lucy Daly (now Mrs. Hap Ward), of the famous Daly family of dancers, and I was proud enough to want to prove to her that I could dance to any music ever composed.

A sudden idea came to me—naturally I had to think very fast. Why not try some buck steps? I'd always used two-four melodies for bucking. No sooner thought of than done. I was into my old "Lively Bootblack" routine before I knew it, but without the spread of the jig sand; and besides, I was in a comedy "make-up." The tempo was very slow, so, in order to make the steps fit, I had to drag them out more or less, and so exaggerated the thing by leaping from one side of the stage to the other instead of sticking to the center.

The melody suggested comedy, so I made every move as eccentrically as I could. I did a jump with the "scissors grinder" step, and threw my head back at the same time. It got a scream of laughter. I repeated this a moment later, and got a second big laugh. Every time I threw my head back, my hair (which I wore exceptionally long at the time) would fly up and then down over my face, and I'd brush it away and do another throw back and up and down the hair would go again. I faked a couple of funny walks to fit in the spots where I had to eliminate certain steps on account of the slow tempo, and each of the walks got hearty laughs and rounds of applause. I finished with an eccentric walking step, throwing my head back with the hair flying all over my face and made an exit with the end of the strain instead of ending with the old-fashioned "break."

The dance was a sensational hit. Lucy Daly came running back stage after the act and went into ecstasies over the thing.

"That's the greatest eccentric dance ever done on any stage," she declared. It was a golden opinion coming from her.

For twenty solid years I did this same dance to the same music, and this was the stunt which eventually not only revolutionized American buck dancing, but also set the "hoofers" to doing away with jig sand, and letting their hair grow long enough to fall over their eyes.

The "Cohan style" they used to call it. But little did they guess that the thing was nothing more or less than an accident brought about by an orchestra playing a two-four melody instead of a six-eight.

Before the following season was over I had risen from the ranks of the ordinary "hoofers" and had become known as a great eccentric dancer. I've told this incident merely to prove that a certain element of luck creeps into almost every success, especially in the theater world.

The expert "hoofers" used to laugh at the idea of anyone saying that I was a good dancer, while the song writers used to kid the life out of my songs. They tell a story about a buck dancer and a song writer "talking me over" in Union Square one day. The conversation ran as follows:

HOOFER. That guy Cohan can't dance.

SONG WRITER. Go on. What are you talking about? He's a great dancer.

HOOFER. He's nothing of the kind. He may be a good song writer, but that lets him out.

SONG WRITER. Well, I say he's a rotten song writer, but he's a great dancer.

HOOFER. What do you know about dancing?

SONG WRITER. What do you know about song writing?

They got into a fist fight, were arrested and fined ten dollars each.

I heard about this argument, and put an "ad" in the *Clipper* in which I claimed I could dance better than any living song writer, and write a better song than any dancer on earth.

They "laid off" of me after that.

CHAPTER XXI

MY FIRST RETIREMENT FROM THE STAGE

WHEN we got back to New York in April (1896) we tried our luck with the variety agencies again for engagements for the "four act," but no, they were still of the opinion that Josie's "single" was still the only thing we had to sell that was in demand.

"But Georgie put a new dance in the act that was the talk of Buffalo," explained dad.

"Yes, but this is New York City. Buffalo is out in the woods," said Vion, the agent.

That had been my "dope" a few years previously, but they couldn't make me believe it at that moment. The four act was in great shape now, and I was dying to get a shot at a New York audience with the eccentric dance. But there were no variety dates in sight, so we looked about for a road show job.

We were signed to play four parts in a new farce comedy written by Frank Dumont, entitled "On the Go." Charles A. Loder (another

German-dialect road star), who was the owner of the show besides being the featured player, confessed to us, when the first salary night rolled around, that he was "broke," and that if the troupe was to continue its travels it would have to be done under a commonwealth arrangement.

Two weeks later the show stranded in Mannington, West Virginia, where I made a speech to the company that if the author had listened to my suggestions and hadn't been too vain to allow me to "fix up" the play, I could very easily have turned it into a huge success. They applauded and cheered me when I made this statement, but I found out years afterward that they were "kidding."

A few weeks later we joined another road show headed by Lydia Yeamans Titus. We opened with this troupe in Cleveland, and after a good week's business the manager jumped out with the bank roll, so we once more went along on the commonwealth arrangement, and the following Saturday night, in Tiffin, Ohio, we stranded again. The closing night, I made another speech to this company that if they had given me my own way about the play, I could have fixed it up and easily have saved the situation. More cheers, more applause, more "kidding," too, as I discovered later on.

We came back to New York again and were engaged by still another road star, Edward M. Favor, to support him in a play written by Edith Sinclair (Mrs. Favor). It was a comedy called "The Jester."

During the second week of the engagement Favor handed us our two weeks' notice, and as he did so I heard him say to dad:

"Jerry, I wouldn't put up with that kid of yours if this show depended on him. Take my advice and put him on a schoolship or send him to jail. I don't care a damn what you do with him, but for Heaven's sake, take him away from me."

"I don't see why he's sore at me," I said to dad, after listening to a long lecture on the "mending of my ways." "I've certainly tried to be a regular fellow with him," I continued. "I even went so far as to offer to fix the play up free of charge."

"These people don't want their plays fixed up. What's the matter with you?" he yelled at me. "Will you, for the love of all that's good and

JERRY J. COHAN AND GEORGE M. COHAN

A SCENE FROM "BROADWAY JONES"

sensible, get on to yourself and quit talking about changing people's plays around?"

"You're not losing faith in me, are you, dad?"

"Yes, I am," he returned. "I'm losing faith in your ever being anything but a 'pest.'" And to add strength to this statement, he slammed the lid of his trunk down with a smash and walked out of the room.

That night I started work on a new poem entitled

"ENCOURAGEMENT"

The first few lines ran:

It was my father's belief in me
That led me to prosperity.

I figured I might need it in case dad failed to cool down.

For the fourth time that year we journeyed back to New York, and after a long stretch of idleness arrived at the conclusion that, as far as the four act was concerned, it was a dead issue. It looked as though we were never going to get the chance to show it in the big city and my new eccentric dance was to go into the discard forever. We decided to let Josie go back to her single dancing specialty, mother and dad were to accept engagements for their sketches, and I was to stick to the writing game. This meant, of course, that I was "through" as a trouper.

I announced to the gang in Union Square (and it was with a heavy heart, believe me), that, owing to the demands made upon my time in other directions, I had decided to permanently retire from the stage.

"You mean you're not going to be a 'trouper' any longer?" inquired a member of a trick bicycle family.

"That's precisely what I mean." I tried to smile as I asserted this.

"Gee! That's going to put an awful 'crimp' in the show business," remarked a wise-cracking hoofer standing near by.

The bunch had a good laugh at this, and I tried to toss it off in an indifferent manner, but I was "hurt" just the same, and as soon as I could gracefully do so, I slipped away and walked through Irving Place.

"I wonder why he pulled that speech?" I juggled the thing around. "I wonder if I'm a 'ham'." I started to sum myself up. "Maybe I've been a joke right along without knowing it."

I wasn't sympathizing with myself at all; I

was honestly trying to weigh things and figure out just where I stood.

"That's funny," I thought. "I always had the idea that I was a pretty good performer"—a little deeper thought now. "But that guy would never have cracked a thing like that to a real trouper."

I took a bird's-eye view of all I had done on the stage—sort of a panoramic *résumé* of my "trouping."

"Maybe he's right. I guess I'm a 'ham,' all right." And I began thinking harder than I ever had in all my life. After a half hour's reflection of the matter, during which I stuck to the side streets, where no one I knew would be likely to catch me doing battle with the teardrops, I started back to the boarding house for the sole purpose of sneaking off to my room, where I could cry to my heart's content and have the thing out with myself once and for all.

One point I had already absolutely decided upon. I was never going to walk on a stage again as long as I lived.

Two minutes later something happened. Yes, sir, something happened that changed my ideas all around. Aladdin swung his lamp and the Cohan luck peeped over the wall.

As I opened the front door of the boarding house, I heard dad sing out, "Here he is, now." I looked up and saw him flying down the stairs, followed by mother and Josie, all three carrying hand luggage, advertising the fact that they were starting out somewhere in a fearful hurry.

"We've been trying to locate you for an hour," continued dad as he pushed by me, reopened the front door, and shooed us all out. "Come on. We've got to get over to Brooklyn as quickly as we can. We open there this afternoon in the four act."

"Zipp's Casino again?" I stopped to ask.

"Zipp's Casino nothing. Hyde and Behman's this time, my boy. Come on." And the four of us started scooting toward the Third Avenue Elevated station at a mile-a-minute clip.

"Hyde and Behman's? Are you kidding, dad?" I was out of breath, trying to keep up with him, but was anxious to hear what it was all about.

"Never mind. I'll explain later. We play

Hyde and Behman's. That's good enough, isn't it?"

"How did it happen?" I whispered to Josie, as we sprang up the Elevated stairs two steps at a time.

She was too winded to answer. I grabbed mother's arm and helped her along. She was about "all in."

"Here comes a train! Hurry! Let's make it," shouted dad, and we flew through the gate out to the platform and aboard the express on our way to what proved to be the turning point in the family career.

CHAPTER XXII

I BECOME A BUSINESS MANAGER

ON the way to Brooklyn, dad explained to me that Filson and Errol (then one of the leading sketch teams of the country) had received word that morning that Mrs. Filson's mother, who lived in Chicago, had been taken dangerously ill and that they had been forced to cancel their engagement at Hyde and Behman's and start West immediately.

It was their place in the bill we were being rushed into, and it was through the great friendship existing between Filson and Behman that the thing had been arranged. It was the first time in many a day that an act which had appeared at any opposition house in Brooklyn had been booked at Hyde and Behman's.

Our case was a most unusual one, too, owing to the fact that we had been very closely identified with "Zipp's." We realized this, and also knew that it would come as a great surprise to everybody around the Adams Street Theater.

Our reception wasn't any too cordial when we arrived there that day about thirty minutes before matinée time.

"Here come the beer-hall favorites now," we heard one of the performers remark as we walked in the stage door. We expected this sort of thing and were set for it.

On the way from New York we had agreed to let all "side speeches" and cutting remarks go by default, knowing in our hearts that if we were lucky enough to "make good" with the audience, all past performances would be quickly forgotten and we'd take our place in the list of regular Hyde and Behman acts.

"The bill's been shifted around. You folks will have to hurry and dress. You open the show." This was the greeting from the stage manager.

"I thought we were in Filson and Errol's spot?" I put this to him very meekly.

"Never mind what you thought. I'm telling you that you open the show. The orchestra's waiting downstairs in the music room to rehearse your stuff. You can just about make it if you hurry."

The four of us stood staring at one another

in utter dismay. The thought flashed through my mind. "They're trying to get us to quit and walk out." Then a second flash. "Well, we'll fool them." I winked at dad and mother, gave the high sign to Josie, and then turned to the stage manager.

"All right, colonel. Anything you say. You're the doctor."

We ran downstairs, rehearsed the music, and then skipped to our dressing rooms as fast as we could. Dad and I had a hurried talk while we were making up, and decided that we'd go through with the thing at all costs. The folks were astonished at my attitude in the matter, expecting, of course, that I'd fly up and refuse to play, but for some unknown reason I couldn't help thinking that it was all for the best. I kept saying to myself: "This is the best thing that ever happened. Everything's going to turn out all right." And subsequent events proved that I had the thing "tabbed" to a nicety.

"That's a tough spot they're handing you, kid," said George Reno, the contortionist, as I passed him in the hall on the way to the stage to arrange our side props.

"Oh, we don't mind. We're satisfied. We're

tickled pink to be here. We'd rather open the show at Hyde and Behman's than be a star act at any other house." I said this loud enough for everybody back stage to hear.

I'd made up my mind, as long as we were accepting the situation at all, to swallow it hook, line and sinker. I discovered very quickly that these tactics brought about a pretty good result. Even the stage manager's "high and mighty" manner seemed to change.

"Anything we can do for you?" he inquired as I rushed about the stage, preparing things generally for the act.

"Not a thing in the world," I replied, "except to 'root' for us, if you will. We know what it means to make good here. It's been the ambition of our lives to break in with Hyde and Behman."

"Well, go right after them. That's all you've got to do," and he slapped me on the back by way of encouragement.

I noticed out of the corner of my eye that he had stopped and whispered to a group of stage hands on his way to the first entrance, and a moment later they were all rushing about, assisting me in every possible way, and seemed over-anxious to do everything they could to get the act off to a good start.

The overture struck up and the four of us walked up and down the stage as nervous as a quartette of amateurs at a strawberry festival. Not having played the act in some time, we kept muttering lines of dialogue and reminding one another of this or that piece of business, while Slafer's orchestra (which for years was one of the big features at Hyde and Behman's) blasted a selection from the opera of "William Tell."

We were on edge—up on our toes—the biggest moment we had ever known. Hyde and Behman's at last. Everything depended on that first performance. While our great hopes of the future danced before our eyes, the music suddenly came to a stop and we heard a voice announcing in front of the drop curtain:

"Ladies and gentlemen, owing to the sudden cancellation of Filson and Errol, there will be a change in the program. Number one has been shifted to number two, and, as an added attraction, the Four Cohans will open the bill."

To the great surprise of everybody concerned, a solid round of applause followed this announcement. Filson and Errol being particularly big favorites in Brooklyn, we naturally looked for some sign of disapproval on the part of the audience.

"I guess they remember you from Zipp's," whispered one of the stage hands.

I was too flabbergasted to reply to this. I just stood there, shaking from head to foot with genuine stage fright, as the curtain rose to the opening music of our act.

"Goggles Doll House" had always been a seventeen-minute skit. We'd played it often enough to know the running time, but with laughs, encores, and extra calls, we were checked up for exactly twenty-six minutes at the matinée that day.

"Some hit, folks, some hit," the stage manager shouted over the applause as he waved us back to the stage for what he thought was to be our final call.

We started for our dressing rooms, mother and Josie throwing their arms about dad's neck and carrying on a "kissing bee" as we went. When I saw this, I joined in the celebration by executing several buck steps that carried me to the back wall of the theater.

"That opening act murdered 'em," I heard a

song-and-dance man say to his partner as they "limbered up" in one of the rear corners.

"You sure did lay them out and place lilies in their hands, Georgie," the property man yelled to me as he rushed by to prepare for the following act.

The applause continued—gallery cat calls—uniform stamping of feet. The orchestra kept banging away at somebody's introduction music, but the obstinate audience seemed bent on having its own way about things, and the "riot" was on. We were all so overjoyed and excited that without half knowing what we were doing, we continued on our way to the dressing rooms, and were climbing the stairs to the second landing in the outer hall when the stage manager, out of breath and red in the face, rushed through the swinging doors and shouted at the top of his voice, "The Four Cohans! The Four Cohans! Another bow, please. Quick as you can, please. Hurry! You're holding up this show."

We rushed down the stairs, through the door, to the first entrance and on the stage, in front of the "scene in one" as they used to call the "close in" flats. The applause seemed to increase tenfold as we reappeared, walking hand-in-hand to the footlights to acknowledge this unusual demonstration by what was conceded to be the most exacting and sophisticated variety-show audience in America.

"Speech! Speech!"

Nothing of this kind had ever happened to us before. I turned to dad, expecting him to offer a few words of thanks; but he gave me a nod of the head, so I stepped to the edge of the footlights, raised my hand for quiet, and for the first time in my life, said:

"Ladies and gentlemen, my mother thanks you, my father thanks you, my sister thanks you, and I thank you."

A howl of laughter followed this, and then another rousing round of applause went up as we left the stage.

It was my first curtain speech, and got such a laugh that I never bothered writing any other for the twenty years that followed. The performers and stage hands crowded around us and gave us a little applause on their account.

Everybody seemed as pleased as ourselves. "Nothing succeeds like success." I never got the real meaning of the old saying until that minute.

When we got to the outer hall again, after another four-cornered kissing contest, we joined hands and did a triumphant "ring-around-a-rosie" before we climbed the stairs to the dressing rooms. The whole thing happened so quickly and so unexpectedly that no one realized at the time what a really big hit the act had made.

A few minutes later, while dad and I were sitting on the edge of a trunk in our dressing room, laughing and congratulating each other, a knock came at the door.

"Come in," I called out.

A short, stocky, serious-looking man entered and introduced himself.

"Excuse me, gentlemen," he said. "My name is Henry Behman; I'm Lou Behman's brother (Lou Behman was the head of the firm). He wants to see you folks in his office around the corner in the Park Theater Building as soon as you've 'washed up.' If you want me to, I'll wait downstairs till you're dressed and show you the way there myself."

"We'll be with you in five minutes, Mr. Behman," said dad, and we jumped up and started to dress for the street.

"What do you suppose he wants?" dad whispered as Behman left the room.

"He doesn't want to fire us, that's a cinch." And I did a couple of buck steps over to the wash basin.

"It'll seem kind of foolish for the whole family to go traipsing into his office. Maybe he wants to see only one of us," dad suggested.

"I think you're right, dad. Perhaps it would be a better idea for you to see him alone."

"No," he hesitated. "I'd rather not go there alone."

"Well, then, supposing I go round and see what he wants?" I was aching for the chance.

"Would you mind doing that, son?"

"I should say not. I'll be tickled to pieces." And I hurried all the more for fear he'd change his mind.

My father was a very timid man and always seemed to me to have a holy horror of talking business, especially with theatrical managers. His quiet, gentle manner, and the way they used to take advantage of his "let-well-enough-alone" way of going along, was the thing taught me that aggressiveness was a very necessary quality in dealing with the boys who were out to accumulate the nickels and dimes.

"I think it's about time I took these business worries off of your mind anyway, dad," I remarked as I reached for my hat and headed for the door.

"I wish you would son," he answered, with a smile.

"Yes? Well, it's done. I'm going to begin right now." And away I went.

Five minutes later I was sitting in the private office of L. C. Behman, the biggest high-class variety manager in the country.

"Of course, I'd heard of the Four Cohans," he was saying, "but I never knew till to-day that it was Jerry Cohan and his family that made up the quartette. I recognized your father, though, the minute he walked on the stage."

He offered me a cigar. I took it, but lit a cigarette.

"Why, say!" he went on, "if I had ever guessed who you folks were, I'd have booked you here long ago. I saw your dad in a play called 'The Molly Maguires' before you were born."

"You don't say!" I was pretending to be perfectly at ease, but I was scared stiff.

"And the funny part of the whole thing is," he chuckled, "that he was my favorite actor."

"I'll tell him you said that, Mr. Behman." Through nervousness, I put the lighted end of the cigarette in my mouth, but never batted an eye.

"I want you to tell him," he continued, "and I want you to tell him something else, too. Tell him that the act you folks did this afternoon was one of the biggest hits that ever played the house."

"I'll be sitting in Rockefeller's office some day," I thought to myself when he "pulled" this.

"And if it's agreeable to you folks," he went on, "I'll bring you back here in three weeks' time and make you a headline attraction. What do you say?"

My first impulse was to leap over the desk that separated us and plant a little kiss on his brow, but, being a strictly business person (which I had so suddenly become), I tried to appear unconcerned and merely answered:

"All right, Mr. Behman. Anything you say."

Then followed a short little conversation during which he told me all about the old-time performers that had played under his management. He pointed out various photographs of celebrities, such as Barry and Fay, Hallen and Hart, J. W. Kelly (the rolling-mill man), Ward and Vokes, and many others that adorned the walls of his office.

He offered me another cigar. I took it and lit another cigarette.

"Ask your father to run in and see me during the week. I'd like to say 'hello' to him."

"You bet I will, Mr. Behman."

"Say, see here." He took a good look at me now. "You're a pretty young man to be managing the business end of the act. How old are you, young fellow?"

"I'll be eighteen the Fourth of July," I proudly answered.

"Born on the Fourth of July, eh?" He smiled at this. "You ought to write a song about that."

"I will some day. Good-by, Mr. Behman."

"So long, son."

I started through the door and he called me back.

"Oh, just a second," he said. "I forgot to tell you I've changed that bill around for to-night's performance. You folks will be on fourth."

"Thanks, Mr. Behman."

And I hurried back to the theater, where the folks were waiting, and reported that I had arranged return bookings in three weeks with the thorough understanding that we were to headline the bill. I had fought for a better spot on the current program and had succeeded, after a long argument, in being placed fourth, the star position.

"I told him all about you, dad," I raved on, "and when I mentioned 'The Molly Maguires' he spoke up and said he remembered you very well. I told him I'd bring you around during the week to say 'hello.' "

The three of them stood staring at me as though I were a freak.

"Well, I hope you folks are satisfied now that I'm a pretty good business man." I was looking for compliments and I got them. Dad shook hands with me, mother and Josie kissed me, and we celebrated the happy event with a turkey dinner between matinée and night in Brooklyn's most fashionable restaurant, where it was decided very definitely that from then on I was to be the sole business representative and managing director of the Four Cohans.

CHAPTER XXIII

GETTING TALKED ABOUT

"JIM" HYDE was owner and manager of a famous traveling organization known as "Hyde's Comedians," a combination of vaudeville acts selected each year from the Hyde and Behman bills.

On seeing our performance during the return engagement week, he immediately grabbed us for his company.

"I'll give you the same salary you're getting now," he said. He knew we'd already been offered twice that figure.

"I'll take it, Mr. Hyde." And we shook hands, which was the only contract necessary. A theatrical man's word was not only his bond, but his greatest asset in those days.

The acceptance of this engagement seemed to my folks to be an unbusiness-like move, but I convinced them that a season with this attraction meant more to us than money.

In the company that season (1896) were a

number of headline acts such as Helena Mora, Johnny Wild, McIntyre and Heath, Conroy and Fox, the Newsboys Quintette (which included Gus Edwards, who at that time was a ten-year-old boy soprano), Thorne and Carlton, and several others. We toured with this show for about twenty-five weeks, and when we left (which was because of an argument I'd had with Hyde concerning the way we were billed), we were immediately booked for six weeks' engagement in California. This "time" was to be divided between 'Frisco and Los Angeles. These two houses were the only Orpheum theaters in existence at that time. Since then, however, the Orpheum Circuit, as it is known to-day, covers all the principal cities of the West, from Chicago to the Pacific coast.

Before leaving New York for this engagement, I planted a song for publication, which blossomed into the biggest hit I'd had up to that time. It was a coon march number called "The Warmest Baby in the Bunch." Ragtime marches came thick and fast from that time on.

On the way to 'Frisco, I said to dad, "I'd like to try a couple of new acts during this California trip."

He looked at me in surprise; so did mother and Josie. Up to now, dad had contributed all the material used by the family, and, although I'd kept up my sketch writing and continued to supply others with one-act skits, until then I had never had the courage to suggest doing the Cohan acts.

"What do you mean, a couple of new acts?" dad inquired.

"Read these and let me know what you think of 'em," I said as I pulled the manuscripts from my suitcase and handed them over. I'd written them while with the Hyde show.

"The Professor's Wife" and "Money to Burn" were the titles of these two skits, and, after the first reading, dad not only resigned as the family author, but suggested that "we waste no further time on the old stuff," but get into rehearsals on the train and open with "The Professor's Wife." By the time we arrived in Los Angeles we had the act down dead-letter perfect.

It was a screaming hit and made the Four Cohans California favorites overnight, so to speak.

We followed it up with the second skit, "Money to Burn," the last week of the engagement, and this act (which, by the way, was a fifty-five-minute entertainment) turned out to be one of the biggest hits vaudeville had ever known.

After playing an extra week in 'Frisco, we left there with flying colors and hurried back to New York for our first appearance at Tony Pastor's Theater.

We opened there, and on the bill were such favorites as Favor and Sinclair, Williams and Walker, O'Brien and Havel, Clifford and Huth Wood and Shepard, and two or three other big headliners for the opening program of the season.

We went on Monday matinée at 4.30, and when we left the stage after our final call, it was exactly 5.40 by the first-entrance clock, an hour and ten minutes to the second. "Money to Burn" was a "panic," at least that's the way the variety actors described the thing.

"Pull your trunks in this theater any week you happen to have open," said Pastor, after the matinée. All sorts of propositions flew from every direction. The agents crowded their way into the dressing room, offering unheard-of inducements for the right to our exclusive bookings. I could hardly wait to get to Union Square and hear what the "gang" had to say.

Actors are no different from any other class of people. They're always with a winner; consequently, it was a hand-shaking, back-slapping contest from that time on. I was the center of attraction in variety circles, the original "Here-he-comes-now" kid.

And, oh, boy! how I used to eat it up! If some performer or other failed, as I thought, to "make a fuss over me," he was out of my life forever. I was the "spot light" attraction. The center of the stage or nothing at all.

"Why shouldn't he have a swelled head?" I overheard a fellow in the connecting dressing room say to a performer who'd been roasting me about being "chesty." "Look what he's done," went on my defender. "Written song hits, sketch hits, and now he comes along and knocks 'em cold as an eccentric dancer and low comedian."

"Yes, that's so, too. I never thought of that," agreed my prosecutor. He was evidently convinced. So was I, and from that minute on my set speech was, "Look what I've done—written song hits, sketch hits, and now I come along and knock 'em cold as an eccentric dancing comedian. Give me a little credit, will you?"

To this day I meet old-timers who say: "Gee! I used to hate you when you were a boy. You were the meanest kid ever lived."

"But I was a clever kid, didn't you think so?" I always ask.

"Sure you were clever," they come back. "If you hadn't been, you'd have been choked to death."

During the week at Pastor's we were offered fancy engagements right and left, but I tossed them all aside and signed with Weber and Fields for the Vesta Tilley All-Star Vaudeville Company at about one third the salary we could have received from any other management. My reason for this move was to get a shot at the high-class audiences I knew Tilley would draw, and, besides, the show was booked in the first-class legitimate theaters. My folks gave me quite an argument about my business judgment in the matter, but I contended that whatever financial sacrifice we were making would turn into a fine investment for the future.

I proved my case completely. By the end of

the season (1897) we were conceded to be the biggest "four act" in America.

The Vesta Tilley show included Charles T. Aldrich, Lew Dockstader, the Musical Johnstons, Valmore, the Lamont family, Reno and Richards, the Four Cohans, and Tilley herself. It was the greatest variety combination ever organized in this or any other country and created a new standard of vaudeville.

Amy Leslie, the famous Chicago dramatic critic, called it the "greatest all-star aggregation on earth."

While with the Tilley show, I sent in for publication a coon song, called "I Guess I'll Have to Telegraph My Baby," which swept the country and started the coon-song craze (which the publishers claimed was a dead issue) all over again.

I also wrote and presented to Filson and Errol, as a token of our esteem and gratitude for having engineered our first appearance at Hyde and Behman's, a one-act play called "A Tip on the Derby," which eventually became a vaudeville classic.

During that same season, I also wrote and produced "The Wise Guy" for Hayes and Lytton, which I afterward elaborated into a three-act farce comedy, also a brand-new version and complete new score for "The Hot Old Time," in which Johnny and Emma Ray were starring, and new acts for the Russell Brothers, LeRoy and Clayton and several other lesser lights.

One thing I'll say for myself as a kid author, I never "rested on my laurels." No, sir. It was night and day with me, pencils in every pocket and always on the job.

At the end of the Vesta Tilley season we again jumped to California for a return Orpheum engagement, and presented another new skit, entitled "Running for Office," which not only topped "Money to Burn," but brought us offers of a thousand dollars a week, a salary unheard of in those days for an American act.

On our return to New York I again turned down all the big contracts offered and signed with the Harry Williams Vaudeville Company, a rival organization of Hyde's Comedians, at about half the salary we could have demanded anywhere else. I wanted to show Jim Hyde what he'd missed, and besides, we were to be the headliners of the Williams show. Again my folks complained about my business judgment.

"You shouldn't be vindictive, Georgie," said dad. "We all think you should look at things from a strictly business standpoint.

"That's exactly what I'm doing," I argued, "and if you folks don't like the way I'm managing our affairs, just say so and I'll quit."

"All right, son. Have your own way about it." And the thing was settled.

When the Williams show opened in Chicago in September, 1898, I made a stiff kick to the management about the lettering on the three-sheet posters.

"The Four Cohans should be at least twice as big type as any other act on the bill," I asserted, and I made sure that every member of the company heard me, too.

"It's about time you guys got on to the fact that we're the biggest attraction in the show business."

This speech didn't make any particular hit with the performers, but it evidently impressed the management, because the posters were changed to suit my ideas, immediately.

"Georgie, I wish you wouldn't brag so much about the act," Josie said to me one day in a very kindly way. "You've got everybody talking about the way you carry on."

"Well, that's the idea. I want to keep them talking," I shot back.

"But they're not saying very nice things about you, Georgie," she confided.

This handed me a laugh, and I came back with: "Listen, sis. Between you and me, I don't care what they say about me, so long as they keep mentioning my name."

"I know, but don't you consider friendship at all?" she argued.

"I'm considering nothing but showmanship right now, sis."

And that night I made another kick about the newspaper advertisements.

"Get the name bigger! Get the name bigger!" I demanded. The correction was made right away.

Oh, I was a cute little guy. If you don't believe me, ask any of the old-time variety managers.

CHAPTER XXIV

NAME IN ELECTRIC LIGHTS

WHILE with the Harry Williams show (1898-99) I wrote another one-act play for the family, called "The Governor's Son." This skit I afterward made over into a three-act musical comedy, and it served as the first starring vehicle for the Four Cohans.

I didn't produce the one-act version until a year later, however, as I wanted to take the first shot at it before a San Francisco audience, so waited until we were playing our third Orpheum engagement during the summer of 1900.

The Hyde Show wanted us again for the season of 1899-1900, but I sent word to Mr. Hyde that he hadn't money enough to hire us. Lou Behman sent for me and tried to patch matters up, as the Hyde and Behman offices were bent on having the act.

"Would you play under a personal contract with me?" he asked.

"Not with the Hyde Show," I replied.

"Then how about organizing the 'Behman Show'?" he suggested.

After tossing the idea around in my mind for several seconds, I said: "I'll tell you what we'll do, Mr. Behman. We'll sign with you personally for a vaudeville tour, if you'll agree to produce a musical comedy of mine and star the family the following season."

"That's a bet," answered Behman, and the deal was closed. A nominal salary and partnership arrangement.

The Behman Show, which was actually born out of an argument I'd had with Jim Hyde, turned out to be the most popular vaudeville combination touring the country for the following sixty-odd weeks.

It was during this period that the Broadway managers first started to "flirt" with me for stage material. Klaw and Erlanger offered me a contract to do the first "Rogers Brothers" show. I told them I'd rather not tackle the job.

Weber and Fields sent for me to do burlesques for their Music Hall Company. I turned down the proposition, explaining to them that I didn't know enough about the burlesque game.

Oscar Hammerstein wanted me to collaborate

with him on a musical play for the new Victoria Theater.

"You do the book and I'll compose the music," said Hammerstein.

"I always compose my own music," I replied.

"Your own music, eh? That's what you call it, eh? Well, it's your own as far as I'm concerned. I don't want it." And he laughed me out of his office.

Roland Reed asked me to write an American comedy for his personal use. I said I'd rather wait a few years.

I was getting many a bite, but had no desire to land the big fish, not that I was afraid of falling down, exactly; as a matter of fact, I was thoroughly confident that I could have filled all of these orders to the perfect satisfaction of the public and everybody else concerned, but I was a wise enough kid to realize that I wasn't ready to do such important work as well as I felt it could be done with a little more experience.

"I don't want to write for these other fellows, anyway," I said to dad one day. "If this musical comedy of ours is a hit, I won't need them. I'll write my plays and manage them myself."

"That's a pretty big undertaking, son," said dad.

"No, it's a cinch," I assured him. "Wait till you see."

The Behman Show closed, and we went directly into rehearsals with the three-act musical play. I was marking time, waiting for the big event.

It finally came. February 11, 1901, that was the date. Hartford, Connecticut, the opening stand. The lithographed posters read:

—THE FOUR COHANS—
And Their Company of Comedians
In Geo. M. Cohan's American Musical Comedy
"THE GOVERNOR'S SON"

It seemed to me that all of the show business had been transplanted to Hartford for the *première*. New York managers, road managers, booking agents, playwrights, music publishers, dramatic critics, vaudeville stars, and people from every branch of the theater world shook hands with me in the hotel lobby.

Late in the afternoon, after rehearsal, I slipped off alone to the outskirts of the town to get a breath of air and think things over. After four weeks of rehearsals, and the usual over-anxiety and confinement connected with the preparations of a musical comedy, I was just about down to "whisper weight" and so nervous and excited over the opening, I was on the verge of caving in. I thought to myself as I walked along:

"Well, there it is, boys. I wrote it, composed it, staged it, and produced it (I was Behman's partner in the production), and to-night I'm going to play it. If it's a hit, give me credit, boys; if it flops, blame me and me alone."

I stopped and proudly gazed at one of the big twenty-four-sheet posters plastered on a bill-board. I smiled, walked on, and continued my self-complimentary remarks.

"Well, it's been some struggle," I muttered. "It certainly took me a long time to make it." (I was twenty-two.) I looked at my watch; it was 5.30. In less than three hours they'd ring in the overture; inside of four hours the first-act curtain would be down. Within six hours the performance would be over and the verdict in. This all flashed through my mind as I counted the minutes on the way back to the hotel.

I dined with mother, dad, and Josie in my

parents' room. We wanted to dodge the New York delegation in the hotel café. Very little food, and even less conversation. We were too frightened to eat or talk. Our first real opening night. Our initial appearance as stars of a big musical show. We sat there looking at one another, wondering what minute we'd wake up and find ourselves back in the dime museums.

Between 7.30 and 8 o'clock, the entire city of New York walked in and out of my dressing room. At least, it seemed that way to me.

"Good luck, kid."

"Stand them on their heads, Georgie."

"Teach 'em how, young fellow; teach 'em how."

Handshakes, back slaps, good wishes, and "God bless yous" all over the place.

"Ring in the overture." I heard the call.

"Everybody downstairs, please," the stage manager shouted.

I pushed through the dressing room crowd and rushed to the stage, where the company had gathered for final instructions.

"Ladies and gentlemen," I began, as they grouped about me, all dressed and ready for the first act, "don't wait for laughs. Side-step encores. Crash right through this show to-night. Speed! Speed! and lots of it; that's my idea of the thing. Perpetual motion. Laugh your heads off; have a good time; keep happy. Remember now, happy, happy, happy. Do you all understand?"

"Yes, sir," answered fifty voices in unison.

"And don't forget the secret to it all," I added. "Speed! a whole lot of speed!"

A roll of the drums, a pistol-shot. Bang! And the overture was on.

I ran back to the dressing room (now deserted), slammed the door closed, leaned against the make-up shelf, and burst into tears.

CHAPTER XXV

COHAN AND HARRIS

"THE Governor's Son" proved to be a very popular road show. Even Boston, Philadelphia, and Chicago welcomed the little play with open arms, but New York— But that's another story.

The Sunday before our opening at the old Savoy Theater in Thirty-fourth Street, the clerk at the office desk of the Sturtevant Hotel said to me, as I registered that morning:

"Guess you won't be able to open to-morrow night, will you?"

"Certainly we'll open to-morrow night. What's the idea?" I thought he was stringing.

"Don't you folks belong to the White Rats Association?" he inquired.

"What's that got to do with it?" I was half wise now.

"Well, they're going to strike to-morrow. They claim they're going to close up every show that any one of their members is in."

"Oh, that only affects the vaudeville houses," I explained. "We're in musical comedy now."

"No, they're going to close you up, too. I heard them talking about it here in the office last night."

When he said this I hurriedly unfolded a Sunday paper I had under my arm, and, sure enough, on the front page of the news section, the first thing my eyes lit on was a two-column headline, reading, "ALL WHITE RATS ON STRIKE TO-MORROW."

The White Rats was a society of vaudeville actors founded by George Fuller Golden and had been formed to oppose a group of managers who had organized themselves into a body known as the Vaudeville Managers' Protective Association.

I tried to get in touch with George Golden, who was the White Rat president, but he was not to be disturbed. He had presided at an all-night session of the Rat council, and had left orders at his hotel not to ring his telephone until noon. I looked at my watch; it was only 9.30.

"No use in looking around for actors at this hour," I muttered to myself; "they're all asleep."

I had called an eleven-o'clock rehearsal at

the Savoy, so went directly there to wait for the members of the company to arrive. As I walked in the stage door, the old watchman asked, "Are you Mr. Cohan?" I told him I was.

"Go right out to the front office. Hyde and Behman's Theater has been trying to get you on the telephone."

I ran through the auditorium, and a fellow sweeping the front lobby directed me to the box-office phone.

"Hello! Is that you, Georgie?" It was Lou Behman's voice.

"Yes, Mr. Behman. How are you?"

"What are you folks going to do about this White Rat proposition?"

"Don't know a thing about it."

"Well, I'll tell you one thing I know about it," he shouted. "If you or any other member of that company walks out to-morrow night, you'll stay out for good and all."

"Well, now, wait a second. Don't get excited. Let me tell you where I stand, will you?"

"I've already told you where you stand. We'll let it go at that." And he must have hung up the receiver because the connection was gone.

"I'm in a pretty pickle," I thought to myself.

A SCENE FROM "BROADWAY JONES"

GEORGE M. COHAN IN "A PRINCE THERE WAS"

Every member of my company was a White Rat. I ran back stage and met Hughey Mack, who had just walked in the back door. Mack was a member of the Olympia Quartette, who played four important parts in the play.

"I want to see you a minute, Hughey," I said.

"I want to see you, too. I missed you at the hotel," he explained. "I just came from there." We got over in a corner and discussed the matter.

"We'll have to walk out if we're called," he declared, after making me understand that he was speaking for the entire company with the exception of the Cohans.

"But you can't walk out on one of your own members," I protested. "I'm part owner of this show."

"I know, but Lou Behman is a vaudeville manager and we've got to prove our strength," he asserted.

"Do you want me to lose everything I've worked for all my life?" I had already told him of Behman's ultimatum over the phone.

"I'm sorry, kid," he said, "but that's the way it's got to be."

After rehearsal that morning, I ran into Dave

Montgomery, who was vice-president of the Rats.

"Are they going to close up Weber and Fields' Music Hall?" I inquired.

"No. That's not a vaudeville house," said Dave.

"Neither is the Savoy Theater," I protested.

"But Hyde and Behman are vaudeville managers," he argued.

"So are Weber and Fields."

"But they're members of the Rats."

"So are the Four Cohans," I shot back.

"Well, maybe we can fix it up some way. At any rate, don't start worrying until you have to. We'll send word and tell you exactly what to do to-morrow night."

Later in the day I found George Golden and put it up to him.

"What are you going to do with us, George?" I asked.

"Won't know definitely till to-morrow's meeting," he answered. "In the meantime, stand ready to walk out if you're called."

I trotted around town like a madman. All our hopes, all our work, everything we'd struggled for and built up, was about to be toppled over and destroyed on the eve of our first real New York opening.

It was exactly five minutes of eight, Monday night, before we were officially notified that, "owing to the fact that George M. Cohan was a partner in the show, 'The Governor's Son' Company, the White Rat council had decided, was exempt."

It was the toughest experience I'd ever been through, and I was a mental wreck when the curtain rose on the opening act.

The performance that night was, as I've always maintained, "the worst we ever gave." The nervous strain we'd been under for the previous thirty-six hours told its own story in the lack of spirit and dash which were the real essentials of "The Governor's Son." To top this off, I sprained my ankle in the opening number and had to limp through the balance of the play.

"Back to the woods where you belong." That was the general verdict of the New York critics. BROADWAY HAD TURNED THUMBS DOWN, and so, after six weeks of meager business, we packed up our belongings and returned to the road, presenting the same piece until the spring of 1903.

In the meantime, Lou Behman had died and I had acquired his interest in the production. I next turned my old vaudeville skit, "Running for Office," into a three-act musical play and opened at the Fourteenth Street Theater for a spring engagement. This was really our first New York hit and we played there for several months to capacity business. Fourteenth Street, however, was far enough away from Broadway to give me something to still shoot at, and that was the bell I wanted to ring.

During this engagement I received a letter from David Belasco, asking me to call and have a chat. I was at his office at ten o'clock the following morning.

"Mr. Belasco hasn't arrived as yet," explained Ben Roeder, his general manager.

"What does he want to talk to me about?" I inquired.

"Haven't the slightest idea," said Roeder. "Supposing you stroll in later in the day?"

"All right, I will." And I breezed out. When I got to the sidewalk, I got to thinking the matter over.

"This bird about wants to put me under his management. Well, if there's going to be any managing done, I'll do it myself." That was my decision in the matter and my last visit to the Belasco office. To this day, he has never told me what he had in mind, and I've always been too proud to inquire.

The season of 1903-04 we toured the country with "Running for Office," playing all the principal cities from New York to San Francisco.

Josie had been married now for over two years, and she and her husband (who was also a performer) had decided that being separated was a hardship they could no longer endure. The result was that they had signed a joint contract to appear in one of Klaw and Erlanger's attractions the following season. This arrangement naturally meant the breaking up of the trade mark.

"Why don't you write a play and star yourself, Georgie?" Josie suggested. "Mother and dad would be tickled to pieces to play two parts for you." Then to them, "Wouldn't you, folks?"

"I think that's what you should do," agreed dad.

"So do I," echoed mother, and so it was settled that the season of 1904-05 would find me an individual star.

On the way back from the Coast, I slipped a chorus boy into my part, left the troupe in Vancouver, and got into New York during the early part of April, to lay my plans for the new play.

After a short consultation with A. L. Erlanger, it was understood that I was to open in a Broadway theater the following September.

"What's the name of the piece?" asked Erlanger.

" 'Little Johnny Jones,' " I replied.

"What's it all about?" he inquired.

"Wait till you see it. It's the best thing I've ever done." As a matter of fact, I hadn't done it at all. All I'd thought of so far was the title, and that struck me as being a hundred per cent "box office."

I took desk room in the Miner Lithographing Company's offices in the Sheridan Building at Broadway and Thirty-fifth Street, engaged a cast and chorus, signed agreements with scenic artists and carpenters for the painting and building of the production, ordered costumes, props, and printing, and inside of two weeks' time was all set and ready, with the exception of writing the play. I'd been to London the summer before and had conceived the idea of using the

Cecil Hotel courtyard for one scene and the Southampton pier for another, but beyond that I had given no thought to story, situations, or musical numbers, and was far too busy to get down to actual writing until about ten days before the rehearsal call.

"What you ought to have around you is some fellow who could take the business burdens off your mind," suggested Walter Moore, of the Miner Company, one afternoon as he hopped on the side of my desk for a pow-wow.

"Do you happen to know any manager with a whole lot of money who wants to buy in on a sure-fire hit?" I was half kidding when I said this, but he took it seriously.

"Sure I do. There's a little guy right over there that'll take a chance," and he pointed to Sam Harris, who was at another end of the room, looking over a scene model with A. H. Woods, who was a partner of his in several melodramas at the time.

"Hey, Sam!" Walter called out. "Come over here a minute."

Harris and I started a joke conversation about the matter. It seemed that as we talked along we sort of warmed up to each other. That evening we went to dinner together. The next day we both attended a song writers' outing given by a crowd known as the Words and Music Club. Crossing the ferry on the way back from Staten Island that night, we shook hands (which was the only contract ever existing between us) and formed the partnership of Cohan and Harris.

CHAPTER XXVI

THE SPOTLIGHT

WHEN I got through with the manuscript of "Little Johnny Jones" I had an old-fashioned comedy melodrama "all dressed up" in songs and dances.

"You can't play a mob scene, shoot off guns, and dash from heroics into a musical number. The public will never stand for it," said Theodore Kreamer, a writer of popular melodramas, after witnessing my dress rehearsal.

"Well, it's new, isn't it?"

"Yes, it's new, of course, but—"

"Then at least they'll have to give me credit for trying."

That was the only argument I had to offer.

I was superstitious enough to book Hartford as the opening stand, hoping to follow along the luck of "The Governor's Son." "Little Johnny Jones" was a smashing hit, possibly one of the biggest in the history of American musical comedy.

Our first New York engagement with the piece, nevertheless, was a queer experience. We came into the Liberty Theater, and the opening performance was apparently a sensational success. The indifference of both press and public, however, was so pronounced that after seven weeks of half-filled houses we took to the road, pretty well convinced that New York would have none of it.

We moved to Philadelphia, where the play proved such a popular hit that we were immediately recalled to Broadway, where we reopened at the New York Theater and ran to capacity audiences for weeks and weeks. Of course, this was to a scale of popular prices, but the speculators were on the sidewalk collecting fancy premiums just the same. It was the one and only Broadway "comeback" I have ever known or heard of.

We got busy at once and organized a second "Johnny Jones" troupe and sent it throughout the country while I continued to play New York and Philadelphia, and later on Boston and Chicago. It was what is known as a "freak attraction" from a box-office standpoint, but the critics didn't take very kindly to my personal performance of the title rôle.

"A swaggering, impudent, noisy vaudevillian, entirely out of place in first-class theaters," was the opinion of one of New York's foremost dramatic experts. Another prominent critic characterized me as "the musical-comedy nuisance." I thought back to the days of the Buffalo *Advertiser,* when I could write my own notices.

An idea struck me. "Why not publish my own sheet and tell the world what a truly great 'author-composer-actor-manager' I really am?" No sooner thought of than done.

In two weeks' time I was shooting throughout the country copies of a four-page, illustrated, bright and snappy, full-fledged newspaper which I namcd *The Spotlight.*

Walter Kingsley, who was then our press representative, had dug up a mailing list three thousand miles long, so we claimed "the largest free circulation of any theatrical publication in the world."

This little sheet was devoted to the interests of George M. Cohan's plays and productions, with a weekly attack on all unfriendly critics in a column which I wrote and signed myself.

What the boys had to say about me before the *Spotlight* appeared wasn't a masher to the stuff they wrote from that time on.

Week after week, I'd go after them.

Week after week they'd come back at me.

This sort of thing went on for a couple of years before they got on to the fact that they had slipped me at least a million dollars' worth of newspaper advertising free of charge.

"I guess that guy doesn't care what we say about him so long as we keep his name before the public." A Toledo critic is credited with this remark.

I could hardly believe at the time that any guy from Toledo could be smart enough to figure it out.

In the meantime, the "Johnny Jones" song hits were being whistled, brass-banded, hand-organed, and phonographed throughout the United States to such an extent that even the musical critics took a shot at me. "Give My Regards to Broadway," "Good-by, Flo," "I'm a Yankee Doodle Dandy," and all the others were "tin-pan tunes," according to the musicianly highbrows.

"Cohan is a disease," wrote one fellow in

Cincinnati, "and the Yankee Doodle fever is spreading far and wide."

"Fly your flag; Cohan's in town," was the caption line of a cartoon of Uncle Sam addressing the populace, drawn by a comic artist in the comical town of St. Louis.

Even the Providence *Journal,* the "home-town Bible," swung on me with "playing on the patriotic sensibilities of the public."

"I'll get even with Providence for this," I said to myself. It was ten solid years before I played the town again.

During one of our "Johnny Jones" engagements at the New York Theater (we played four of them), A. L. Erlanger said to me:

"Think you could write a play without a flag?"

"I could write a play without anything but a pencil." These flippant remarks always made a hit with Erlanger. He never said so, but I could tell.

"Supposing Cohan and Harris and Klaw and Erlanger form a little partnership arrangement," he went on, "and star Fay Templeton in a new play by you?"

"All right, Mr. Erlanger," I replied, "but

if the play turns out to be a hit, you must promise me that Cohan and Harris and Klaw and Erlanger will all chip in, hire a hack, and go out for a good time."

"Why wait till the play's a hit to do that? Why not hire a hack and do it right now?" suggested the head of the theatrical syndicate.

I didn't know at the time whether he was kidding or not. He was known to be a most exclusive and elusive sort of person—a man who stuck to his desk day and night, with no thought for anything but "business." He had always, as I understood it, pooh-poohed the idea of relaxation, and was not a believer in the old adage, "All work and no play makes Jack a dull boy."

"I'll find out whether this guy's on the square about this thing," I thought to myself.

The next day (Sunday) Sam Harris and I, accompanied by William Harris, Frank McKee, Sandy Dingwall, Mark Klaw, Henry B. Harris, Wilbur Bates, Ren Shields, Mason Peters, Freddy Thompson, Jack Welch, and at least fifty others of the Broadway theatrical and newspaper worlds, gathered in front of Erlanger's town house on West End Avenue at ten o'clock in the morning, rang the doorbell, pushed the butler aside, forced an entrance into the library on the main floor, and sang our "club" song, "Sweet Violets, Sweeter Than All the Roses," harmonizing full strength at the top of our voices until the master of the house appeared in his pajamas.

"What the hell's the idea?" demanded Erlanger.

Ren Shields, who had been appointed spokesman, stepped forward and began:

"Mr. Abraham Lincoln Erlanger, we have gathered here to initiate you into the secret order of the Twenty-Three Club. Long enough have you held yourself aloof from the gay dogs of the gay White Way. If in ten minutes' time you are not fully dressed and ready to start with us on our trip to funland, we swear by all that's sacred to destroy every bit of Napoleonic bric-à-brac in the 'joint'." Then turning to the crowd, he shouted, "Out with your watches, men, and we'll time this fellow."

(Business of all unpocketing timepieces.)

And then to me, another command, "Strike the gong, Brother Desmond," and I rang an old-fashioned dinner bell I had carried there for the purpose.

Erlanger took it all good-naturedly and, after giving us a couple of "drinking lessons," he ran upstairs, and returned a few minutes later, dressed and ready for the outing.

When we arrived at Coney Island at nine o'clock that night (we made several stops on the way), Erlanger was hoisted on top of one of Thompson and Dundy's elephants and led into Luna Park by a brass band and the cheering members of this great secret order. Supper was served in the open air, and the lions' cages were pushed as close to the tables as possible.

"The roars of the wild beasts are warning you, Mr. Abraham Lincoln Erlanger, that our secrets are not to be divulged," shouted Ren Shields to the honored guest, as he was making a stab at a chicken salad.

We arrived back in New York at one o'clock the following morning, and, after an impromptu parade up Broadway from Twenty-third to Forty-second Street, we dispersed and went to our various homes. (Some of us got in.)

These outings were a big feature in Broadway theatrical life for many, many Sundays after that, and the Twenty-Three Club membership grew to such proportions that the New York papers frequently spoke of "the new ten-million-dollar clubhouse soon to be erected in Times Square." It cost eighty dollars to join, and two dollars a day for upkeep. Those were the dues decided on, but no one ever knew who paid their dues, to whom they were paid, or what became of the money.

The trick went like this. If a fellow happened to inquire, "What is this Twenty-Three Club I hear so much about?" the answer would be:

"Don't you belong?"

"No."

"Want to become a member?"

"Yes."

"Give me eighty dollars."

The fellow, after forking over the eighty, would usually inquire:

"What do I do now?"

"Not a thing. Just lay aside two dollars a day for upkeep, and we'll send for it when it's needed."

Then the bird with the "eighty" would telephone the gang to meet him at the Knickerbocker bar. The Shuberts "busted" up the club eventually by refusing to join. They were the only guys left we hadn't "nicked" for the eighty.

At any rate, Erlanger had a good time while it lasted, and that was the original idea. No crowd of college freshmen ever romped and played about with more abandon than the Twenty-Three Club boys.

But it was all innocent fun and did a great deal more good than harm.

On one of these Twenty-Three Club outings, Erlanger whispered to me:

"How about that play you said you'd write for Templeton if I went out for a good time?"

The next day I read him the first act of "Forty-five Minutes from Broadway."

We had both kept our promises.

CHAPTER XXVII

MY FIRST FLOP

WE produced "Forty-five Minutes from Broadway" in Columbus, Ohio.

After a few try-out performances, we jumped to Chicago and opened at the Colonial Theater (the renamed Iroquois); this was in September, 1905. The piece scored an instantaneous success and brought the playhouse back into the good graces of Chicago's theatergoers. The "Standing Room Only" sign was displayed in the lobby throughout the entire engagement of four months. After the New York run of the play at the New Amsterdam Theater, we sent the piece back to Chicago again for another four months' run. A solid year was divided between the two cities, and Fay Templeton scored one of the notable successes of her career.

The two song hits of the play, "Mary's a Grand Old Name" and "So Long, Mary," became even more popular than the "Johnny Jones" score, much to the discomfort and annoyance of the music critics. It was a mixed opinion offered by the dramatic critics of the play itself.

For instance, the fellow in Columbus called it "a feeble attempt at musical comedy," while the Chicago *Tribune* proclaimed it "one of the best song plays in twenty years." I ran these two notices side by side in the Chicago papers as a Sunday "ad," and a little later on I was tipped off that the Columbus critic lost his job.

We organized road companies of "Forty-five Minutes" immediately and sent them throughout the country, while the "number one" troupe played the high spots. With the extra "Johnny Jones" companies and the "Forty-five Minutes from Broadway" shows, along with "Running for Office," which we also sent on tour, the booking offices were being kept fairly busy taking care of the Cohan attractions.

During the season of 1905-06, while I was still appearing in the "Jones" piece, I set to work on still another musical comedy, with a star part for myself. The result was "George Washington, Jr.," in which I opened at the Herald Square Theater early in February, 1906. "Just another Cohan flag-waving affair" was the way the critics summed it up, but the public (God bless 'em) kept lining up at the box office with cash in hand for the balance of the season, while the entire population of New York City whistled "I Was Born in Virginia" and "The Grand Old Flag" with so much delight and enthusiasm that several music publishers accused me of having placed the whole town under salary.

Extreme hot weather brought the Herald Square engagement to an end in June, when, for a summer vacation, I moved to the New Amsterdam Roof Garden, where I revived "The Governor's Son" with all new songs and dances, running on there until the last week in August.

One night during the roof engagement, Nat Goodwin (who was always my favorite American comedian, by the way) came back stage to shake hands and say "hello!"

"Why don't you write a play for me?" he asked.

"Why don't you ask me to?" I replied.

"I'm asking you now," said Goodwin, and a few days later I read the first act of "Popularity" to Sam Harris.

"If you can get two more acts as good as that one, you'll have a hit," declared Harris.

I wired Goodwin and we came to terms by telegraph. It was all settled. The scare headline in the next issue of the *Spotlight* read:

"I'VE GOT NAT GOODWIN WORKING FOR ME NOW."

An indignant telegram came from Goodwin, calling all bets off. My newspaper comedy wasn't any bigger hit with Nat than it was with the critics.

"All right. If he feels that way about it, I'll finish the play anyway and put some one else in the part," and I started looking about for a Goodwin "type."

Thomas W. Ross, who was appearing in Henry Blossom's "Checkers," was the unfortunate actor chosen. I shot right into rehearsals and opened at old Wallack's Theater, Broadway and Thirtieth Street, where it fell as flat as a fried eggplant and closed at the end of the second week. "Popularity" had proved to be my first unpopular play. Oh, boy! what I didn't call the critics, and the public, too, for that matter!

JERRY J., HELEN F., AND GEORGE M. COHAN

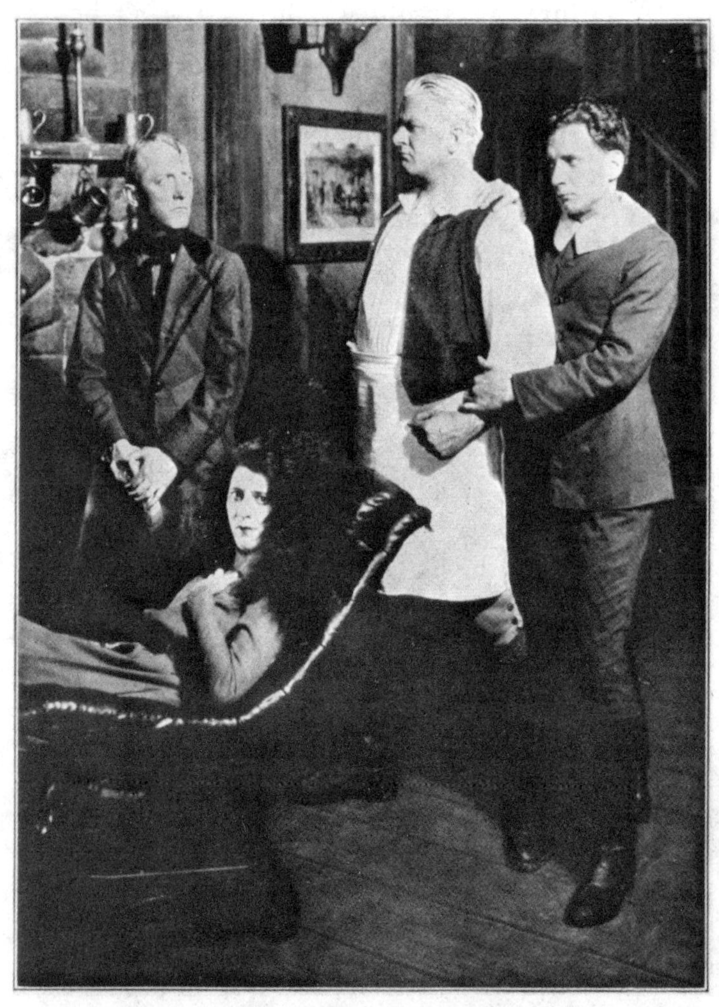

A SCENE FROM "THE TAVERN"

"A failure, an absolute failure! I can't believe it! I won't believe it!" I'd storm to myself. I was fighting mad. No one seemed to offer the right sort of sympathy.

"A few bumps like this will do you a whole lot of good, son," dad said. I couldn't "get" that speech at all.

"The trouble with you, kid," advised Sam Harris, "is that you're trying to do too much."

"Is that so? You think so, eh? Well, let me tell you something, young fellow, I haven't even started to get busy yet."

I flew back to the hotel and started work on a new idea called "Fifty Miles from Boston." Six weeks later we produced the play in Springfield, Massachusetts, and before the season was over had several companies presenting the piece on tour.

Meanwhile I had taken the incidental music of "Popularity" and blended two of the strains into a march. I published it under the name of "The Popularity March." It was one of the first rag marches to score a popular hit, and, incidentally, paid all financial loss of my share in the ill-fated play. But even this didn't satisfy me. No, siree, I refused to accept failure.

"I'll find some way to make 'em like that piece." I kept repeating this to myself over and over again.

I finally hit upon an idea. But that's another story, or perhaps I should say chapter.

CHAPTER XXVIII

WORKING UNDER ADVICE

IN September, 1906, I started on a tour of the country in "George Washington, Jr.," and didn't see New York again until the latter part of April, 1907. When I returned, however, I carried two play manuscripts under my arm, the results of the steady "grind" I'd kept up during the trip. One was a summer song show called "The Honeymooners," the other a four-act musical comedy written to star Victor Moore, entitled "The Talk of New York."

I immediately went into rehearsals with "The Honeymooners," in which I appeared personally on the New Amsterdam Roof for the entire summer of 1907. At the same time I rehearsed and staged "The Talk of New York." This piece opened at the Colonial in Chicago the last week in August, where it remained until Thanksgiving week, when it was brought to New York for a successful run at the Knickerbocker Theater.

I had fully intended to retire from the stage and devote my time to play-producing at this point, but Henry W. Savage requested me to lend him the services of Donald Brian (who was appearing in "Fifty Miles from Boston" at the time) for the rôle of the Prince in "The Merry Widow." Brian went to Savage and I went into his part in the Cohan piece, in which I remained for several months.

While playing in "Fifty Miles from Boston" I wrote and composed still another musical comedy with a star part for myself. It was called "The Yankee Prince," which I placed in rehearsals in March (1908) and followed "The Talk of New York" into the Knickerbocker in April.

It was in this play that a reunion of the Four Cohans was brought about. Besides dad and mother, for whom I'd written parts, I also engaged Josephine for the dancing heroine, and the billing matter read:

GEORGE M. COHAN and his
ROYAL FAMILY

You should have heard what some of the boys had to say when I "pulled" this line on them.

One critic suggested that the advertising matter should be changed to read, "George M. Cohan and Family Royalties." I don't know yet whether he meant this for a knock or a boost.

It was during the New York run of "The Yankee Prince" that the American dancers unanimously agreed that "that guy Cohan certainly is a wonderful dancer."

I had waited for over fifteen years to hear them say it, and I was the happiest "hoofer" in the world.

In August, 1908, I organized, wrote, and produced what was known as the Cohan and Harris Minstrels. It was (if I do say it myself) the greatest organization of the kind ever put together. The company included George (Honey Boy) Evans, George Thatcher, Eddie Leonard, Julian Eltinge, The Bogany Family, and an ensemble of eighty-odd singers and dancers. We lost over a hundred thousand dollars with this attraction before we discovered that American minstrelsy was a dead issue with the theatergoing public.

While the minstrels were in rehearsal, I wrote and composed a musical comedy called "The American Idea," a companion piece to

"The Yankee Prince." This piece opened at the New York Theater and then made a tour of the country. With these early productions off of my mind, I started on a coast-to-coast trip in the "Prince" piece, and my travels continued until April, 1910.

When I got back to New York that spring, I went into rehearsals with a new musical play I had written for Raymond Hitchcock. It was called "The Man Who Owns Broadway"; it was a musicalized version of "Popularity," the Wallack's Theater fiasco. Bang! It went over with a smash. My slate was clean; I'd wiped out the only failure I'd ever known. You should have read the *Spotlight* that week! Hitchcock made an enormous hit in this piece and continued in the part for two solid years.

"Better stick to musical comedy, kid," my friends advised. "Popularity" proved to them that I'd never write a successful play without music. On the strength of this advice, I bought the dramatic rights of George Randolph Chester's "Get Rich Quick Wallingford" stories, and turned them into a four-act play which I opened at the Gaiety Theater in September, 1910, where it remained until the Cohan Theater (which was being constructed at the time) was ready for occupancy. We made the shift in February to the latter house, and when the engagement ended I had the satisfaction of having had a year's run on Broadway with a play of mine without a song or note of music. This piece was afterward produced in every English-speaking country in the world. It was also translated into French and given a Paris production.

"Don't ever waste your time on a musical play again as long as you live," advised most of the boys after the "Wallingford" production. On the strength of this advice, I sat down and wrote the book and music of "The Little Millionaire," in which I personally opened the following September, 1911. I "coppered" every bet they made on me and always tried to do the unexpected.

By now, Cohan and Harris were looked upon as about the busiest little theatrical firm in the game. We had not confined our managerial efforts to Cohan plays, by any means. We were starring John Barrymore in "The Fortune Hunter," Laurette Taylor in "The Girl in Waiting," E. J. Dodson in "The House Next Door," and Wallace Eddinger and Douglas Fairbanks in the New York and Chicago companies of "Officer 666." We had also become partners with Klaw and Erlanger in the Grand Opera House, the Gaiety, and the George M. Cohan theaters and had in construction the Bronx Opera House at 149th Street. We had also come into control of the Chicago Grand Opera House, and a little later took over the lease of the Astor Theater at Broadway and Forty-fifth Street. At least a dozen one-night-stand theaters were also on our list of enterprises, so, all together, we were anything but gentlemen of leisure.

I kept up my trouping just the same, besides writing, composing, reading plays, and running from one rehearsal to another, day in, day out, year after year, without a let-up of any kind.

During the spring of 1911 I was elected to membership in the Friars Club, and to celebrate the event proposed and arranged an all-star frolic, with a cast including William Collier, Richard Carle, Julian Eltinge, Lew Dockstader, Andrew Mack, James J. Corbett, George Evans, Tom Lewis, Irving Berlin, Fred Niblo, Emmett Corrigan, George Beban, William Rock, Raymond Hitchcock and dad and myself, along with sixty others in the ensemble. We toured the principal cities from New York to Chicago and brought back a bank roll big enough to purchase the cornerstone which we laid for the splendid monastery the Friars now occupy in Forty-eighth Street.

During this trip I put the finishing touches on a comedy I was writing, called "Broadway Jones." I went into the title rôle myself and opened at the Cohan Theater in September, 1912. It was my first appearance in a "straight" part on Broadway.

After two hundred and fifty performances of this piece on Broadway, I jumped to Chicago for a summer run, while a second company presented the play on tour.

"Broadway Jones" was also successfully produced in both England and Australia. Seymour Hicks appeared in the title role during the London season. The story was also novelized and afterward made into a highly profitable motion picture.

During the Chicago run of the play I worked on a dramatization of Earl Den Bigger's novel, "Seven Keys to Baldpate," and brought the completed manuscript back to New York in time for the August rehearsals. We opened "Baldpate" at the Astor Theater in 1913. *The panic was on.*

Help! Murder! Police! Cries of anguish. Roars of disapproval. Critics, playwrights, Drama Leaguers, and literary ladies and gentlemen of all sorts, sizes, and standing stood on their hind legs and denounced the dramatization instanter.

"He's tearing down traditions."

"He's breaking all rules and regulations of play construction."

"He's insulting the intelligence of the public."

The entire regiment aimed and fired.

"What's the matter? What have I done?" I innocently inquired of a well-known playwright who had attended the opening night performance.

"You know what you've done, don't you?"

"I certainly do not," I confessed.

He looked at me with pity.

"On what lines have you usually constructed your plays?" he asked.

"Mostly on the Pennsylvania and New York Central," I replied.

He immediately reported to the "circle" that Cohan was a hopeless "hick."

The public flocked to "Baldpate." They came in hacks and packs and stacks. Capacity at the Astor for the entire season. Another company presented the play in Chicago. Same thing out there. All farce records broken.

A few months later, an editorial writer called it a masterpiece of play construction. I was immediately elected to membership in the Dramatists Club. Later on, they made me president. Percy Mackaye suggested that I build a theater for Harvard College dramatic students and perpetuate my name and fame.

I thought the matter over and decided to build. But not in Cambridge. I switched the location to Long Island and made it a home instead of a theater. It's a cute little home, too. Ask any critic.

CHAPTER XXIX

COMING INTO MY OWN

IN October, 1913, with all the shows going and the season off to a good start, I again took to the road as a "trouper," making a tour of the principal cities in "Broadway Jones." This trip came to an end in Detroit, Michigan, January 31, 1914, my dad's sixty-sixth birthday.

I made him a partner in all my theatrical enterprises and announced our permanent retirement from the stage. Mother and dad made good their threat. They never appeared again. A combination of circumstances, however, led me back to the footlights in a very short time.

I hustled back to New York from Detroit and began wading through a mountain of submitted play manuscripts that littered the Cohan and Harris desks.

I immediately became what is known as a "play doctor." Rewriting, reconstructing, and generally revising 'scripts that contained some outstanding idea.

With Carlyle Moore, I worked on a farce called "Stop Thief!" which, after several "try-outs" of several versions, we finally brought into the Gaiety Theater. It turned out to be a very popular farce success. A few weeks later I bought from a popular magazine the stage rights of a story called "None As So Blind"—at least that was the title used on the galley sheets. I notified the magazine that I was going to call the play version, "The Miracle Man," so they published the story under that title, also. I worked on the dramatization of this yarn for over two months before I completed the 'script. Up to then I had never devoted more than three or four weeks to any one play of mine.

We opened "The Miracle Man" at the Astor Theater early in September, 1914. The piece, while not a great box-office success, brought out several fine individual performances, notably the bit of character work done by Frank Bacon (who later became the star of "Lightnin'" as the small-town hotel-keeper).

Around the holiday time I sold the motion-picture rights of the play, handed the production over to the stock companies, and started looking about for an attraction to follow along at the Astor.

"I'm stuck up for a show, Willie. Would you hop in a play right away, if I wrote it?"

I said this to William Collier at the Friars Club one afternoon.

"I'll hop in it if you will," replied Willie.

"But I've sworn I'd never act again," I explained.

"You never did," he came back.

"Listen, Willie," I returned, after he had scored his laugh with the "gang." "I've caught you making believe you're an actor, and I never thought you were so good yourself."

"I'm terrible, I know that," said Collier, "so let's go in a play together, and find out which is the worst."

We agreed to this with a handshake.

"I'll go home now and start work on the first act." And I headed for the club-house door.

"Make it sure-fire, kid," Willie sang out. "Put a couple of flags in it."

The following Monday we were in rehearsals with a musical review called "Hello, Broadway!" in which we opened Christmas night. The success of this production is theatrical history. Collier proved himself to be as great a comedian in musical comedy as he was already conceded to be in farce. During this engagement at the Astor, which ran until the hot weather set in, I again went back to play-doctoring, working with Max Marcin on a melodrama called "The House of Glass." When that was completed, I started work on an original play for Chauncey Olcott for the following season, and upon finishing that I plunged immediately into a three-act farce which I named "Hit the Trail, Holliday."

Day and night, day and night, grind, grind, grind, besides the eight performances a week of a singing and dancing show, and don't forget that I had other business matters to attend to along with all this.

"You've certainly got things breaking pretty nice for you, young fellow," my friends would say.

"That's right, I realize that I'm a pretty lucky little guy," and I'd be half dead for the want of sleep when I'd say it.

But no one ever heard me complain of the work. No one ever heard me acknowledge that

I was tired. I was always there with the big smile and apparently making light of it all.

The following August, during "The Great Lover" rehearsals, Leo Ditrichstein said to me:

"Why don't you take a trip abroad and rest up a bit?"

"I'll do that little thing," I promised, "just as soon as your play is on."

When "The Great Lover" was successfully launched, I made plans to spend the winter in the south of France and proceeded to prepare for the trip.

"Give us another *revue.*"

"Don't go away until you've given us another *revue.*"

This was shot at me from every direction. European trip immediately canceled.

A hop, skip, and jump to the nearest piano and the old F Sharp chords were properly punished until I had drummed out the second Cohan *revue.* A month later, the show was produced at the Astor Theater, where it scored the biggest kind of success. I got so excited over the hit of this piece that all thoughts of a trip abroad were dismissed and I spent the balance of the winter reading and revising manuscripts, besides doing a little picture-acting on the side.

Plays, plays, plays—mauling over plays of all sizes and subjects. It's a great life, boys, if your eyes hold out and the pencil factories keep open.

During this play-doctoring period Adolph Zukor of the Famous Players Motion Picture Company made me a proposition to appear personally in the picturizations of three of my plays, namely, "Broadway Jones," "Seven Keys to Baldpate," and "Hit the Trail, Holliday." I accepted the offer and wouldn't have missed the experience for worlds.

Over to Fort Lee, back to a New York studio, up the state for an outdoor scene, down to Jacksonville, Florida, for another location. They had me running about the country like a wild man, and during all this I was working on a new version of a comedy called "The Tailor-Made Man," which was about to be placed in production.

I think my contract with the picture people was the biggest they had ever written up to that time. It took ten weeks' work to make the three plays, and I received exactly $30,000 a week for my services. I was dizzy from high-power lights and travel, but I came right back and dashed into the rehearsals of "The Tailor-Made Man."

It was in this piece that Grant Mitchell first appeared as a star. This little comedy by Harry James Smith proved a smashing hit and ran for an entire year at the Cohan and Harris Theater. Several months more of play-reading followed this production, along with the supervising of a couple of new shows in rehearsals. I had drifted away from musical comedy altogether by now, and never thought of sitting at a piano.

The day we declared war on Germany, however, I fooled around the F Sharp chords long enough to turn out a little war song, and a few months later the song writers said for the first time, "That guy Cohan certainly can write a song." I'd waited a long time to hear them say this, but it took an upheaval of civilization to bring the thing about.

Little by little, you've probably noticed that I came into my own. Accepted by the dancers in 1908, "okayed" by the Dramatists in 1913, and taken into the fold by the song writers in 1917.

Of course, they didn't any of them hand me any medals or loving cups or anything like that;

they merely told in their own language that I "belonged." I've always thought that the least they might have done would have been to slip me a red, white, and blue ribbon, or something of the kind.

You see, I'd like to be able to prove to the layman that I'm in high society.

"Now, if they'd only admit that I'm a good actor," I thought to myself.

But, alas! the actors refused to declare themselves.

CHAPTER XXX

NO VACATIONS

"I WANT you to do a favor for me, Georgie," said George Tyler, the genial theatrical manager, during the spring of 1918. I thought surely he was going to ask me to rewrite a play, but he explained that he wanted me to play in one, instead.

"I'm promoting an all-star tour for the benefit of the American Red Cross Society," he continued. "It's two weeks' hard work, but it's for a worthy cause."

"Sure. Put my name down," I said, and he handed me the rôle of the invalid American soldier in Hartley Manners' war play, "Out There."

The cast included Mrs. Fiske, Laurette Taylor, Madame Cisneros, Helen Ware, Julia Arthur, James K. Hackett, James T. Powers, H. B. Warner, George Arliss, George McFarland, Chauncey Olcott, O. P. Heggie, and several others. We turned all the big cities into one-night stands, and returned to New York in two weeks' time, after playing to gross receipts amounting to over six hundred thousand dollars.

It was without exception the most successful all-star affair ever put together. It was from a box-office standpoint, at any rate. As for the company, well—it was just like a great big family. Have you ever lived next door to a great big family? If so, you've possibly some idea of what I mean. Laurette Taylor wrote a book about the trip. I could have written several, but I laughed them off.

While on this trip I wrote a new play for Chauncey Olcott, "The Voice of McConnell," which we put into rehearsals upon our return to New York. In this play Olcott did the best light-comedy work of his career.

Again I announced the fact that I was about to grab a boat for sunny France. I was bound to get that long-waited-for vacation in some way, some time or other.

"Give us another *revue.*" "Don't go away until you've given us another revue." Special request of the boys and girls of Broadway. European trip postponed.

"Bring on your darned old piano," I cried, and sat down and tried to work. I was all in, dead tired, and for the first time in my life acknowledged the fact, but only to myself. My mind was dull, the piano seemed out of tune, or out of sympathy, I couldn't tell which. The melodies were commonplace, the lyrics were worse. "What'll I do?" I thought.

An idea flashed in my mind. I ran to the telephone.

"Get Irving Berlin on the wire," I hollered, and waited for the connection.

"Hello, Irving! How'd you like to do a *revue* with me?"

"I'll be right over," he sang back.

Together we drummed out the troupe which opened at the New Amsterdam Theater, Christmas night, 1918. This show, with Nora Bayes heading the cast, finished out the season in New York and then made a tour of the principal cities. With this production off of my mind, I sat down and gave myself a good talking to.

"You've been going pretty strong, young fellow, for over thirty years, without relaxing at all. You'll fall in a heap the first thing you know." Then a little further thought on the subject. "Take a long rest, kid. The whole thing isn't worth the worry." While laying down the law to myself along these lines, I opened a package that had just arrived by mail.

It contained an autographed photograph of President Wilson: "To George M. Cohan from Woodrow Wilson," it was inscribed.

"What's this all about?" I wondered.

An inclosed note fell to the floor. It read:

> Dear George Cohan: The President considers your war song, *"Over There,"* a genuine inspiration to all American manhood.

The note was signed by the President's secretary, Joseph P. Tumulty.

I started thinking again, but along different lines.

"The whole thing isn't worth the worry, eh?" I looked at the President's signature again. "You were going to quit, were you?" I read the note over the second time. "We'll see about that."

I hurried to the safe, where I secreted the secretary's note, placed the President's photograph on my office desk, sat down, and started work on a new version of a play called "The Acquittal."

There I was, right at it again. The vacation stuff just wasn't in the cards.

CHAPTER XXXI

STEVE REARDON

I HAD just finished the second act of "The Acquittal" when I received a hurried call for help from Robert Hilliard. I threw aside the manuscript I was working on and rushed to his assistance.

Little did I suspect what a cute little "jam" I was getting myself into when I hopped on a train for Philadelphia to offer an opinion on a played called "A Prince There Was." Hilliard had produced the piece and was appearing in the leading rôle.

"Close it up, Bob," I advised, after watching the entire performance.

"Isn't there anything good about it at all?" he asked.

"Not from where I was sitting," I replied.

"How do you like the title?" He was trying to interest me from some angle.

"It's a fairly good title," I admitted, "but there's no entertainment in a name."

"Couldn't you take the title and write a play around it!" he inquired.

I laughed at the idea, and explained to him that I was hard at work on a melodrama for early production and couldn't think of such a thing.

"I wish you'd help me out, kid, I'm up against it with this production on my hands. It's cost me a pile of money and for old times' sake I'm going to ask you to stretch a point in my behalf."

He'd put it right up to our friendship, which had been one of years' standing. I had never written or rewritten plays for any office except my own, and, knowing this fact, Hilliard offered to go under my management and hand the production over to do with as I saw fit.

"No, I'd rather not become interested in that way, Bob," I told him, "but just to show you that I'll go through for a pal, I'll write a new version of this thing under a regulation author's contract."

He couldn't begin to thank me enough. His partner in the production, William Elliott, shook hands with me a hundred and fifty times before I boarded the midnight train for New York.

I laid aside "The Acquittal" and went to work on "A Prince There Was." I kept the same set of characters and stuck to the title, but outside of that there was nothing of the original play left when we went into rehearsals ten days later.

The play opened in Stamford, Connecticut, for one night, and then went straight to Broadway and into the George M. Cohan Theater. The press was bad, the business was bad, and the critics all agreed that the play was bad. Friday night of the opening week Hilliard and I had a talk. It started as an argument, but ended in a friendly chat.

"I don't like the part," he said.

"I think it's a great part," I argued.

"The play's all wrong."

"The play's all right, Bob."

"Why don't you play it yourself?" he suggested.

"All right, I will." I wrote him out a check for twenty-five thousand dollars, gave him a share in the future profits, a small percentage of the gross receipts, and hopped in the following afternoon (Saturday matinée) after a twenty-minute rehearsal with the company. The piece

GEORGE M. COHAN AS THE VAGABOND

A SCENE FROM "THE SONG AND DANCE MAN"

remained at the Cohan Theater for the balance of the season and proved a genuine box-office success.

Toward the end of March I slipped Grant Mitchell into the part and quietly stepped out of the cast. We organized a second company of the same piece, which toured the country while the "number one" show played the principal cities. It was during the New York run of "A Prince There Was" that Isidore Witmark, the music publisher, brought me the manuscript of "Cherry Blossoms," a three-act operetta.

"Here's a great little musical play," he said. "I wish you'd look it over."

"How's that old song of mine getting on?" I inquired. He had almost forgotten he'd ever published a song of mine.

"What song is that?" he inquired.

I mentioned the title, " 'Why Did Nellie Leave Her Home?' "

We had a great laugh over the old song and chatted about the old days, and I agreed to read the operetta and let him know within a week whether or not I'd be interested in its production.

The next day I called him on the phone.

"All right, Issy," I said. "I'll do that piece." He was tickled to pieces. So was I.

"Here's where I get even," I thought to myself.

I revamped the score, interpolated a half dozen new numbers, rewrote the book, twisted the story upside down, poked fun at the whole idea, turned the operetta into a jazzy musical show, renamed it "The Royal Vagabond," and produced it at the Cohan and Harris Theater. It was a smashing success and everybody was satisfied. It took me twenty-five years to get even with the Witmarks, and that's the way I did it.

With this show successfully landed, I went back to the unfinished manuscript of "The Acquittal," which I hadn't touched in months. I finished it up in a week's time and placed it in rehearsals at once. "The Acquittal" was a dramatization of a story by Rita Weiman, who sent it to me in play form, and requested that the play be "Cohanized" for production.

After a week in Atlantic City for a tryout which proved successful, we took it off and laid it aside for the following season. It was now June, 1919, and I hadn't a blessed thing on my mind and was to be as free as a bird until September time.

"Nothing to do till September." I could hardly believe it was true.

"Here's a chance for a real vacation at last," I whispered to myself. I got on the phone and rang up Steve Reardon at the Friars Club.

Steve and I had been pals for years. We still are, for that matter.

You might picture Reardon as a tall, slender, delicate-looking individual wearing horn-rimmed glasses and carrying an umbrella under his arm.

You may picture him like that if you care to, but don't let him hear about it.

Reardon is a "cop," or rather he was a "cop" for over twenty years. He was a wonderful "cop," too. Ask any "cop." He's been retired for a long time now, and is a gentleman of leisure in the truest sense of the word. He has a brain, loves books, and possesses a bank roll.

Reardon hasn't worked in years and solemnly swears that he never will again. Can you imagine a man who not only absolutely refuses to work, but goes about advocating the idea, hanging around with me? Well, it's a fact.

Reardon and I string it out together. We get many a laugh, too. He always refers to me as "The Slave," while my pet name for him is "Hobo."

"How about a little motor trip to Chicago?" I asked him over the 'phone.

"What's going on in *Double Newark?"* he inquired. He labeled the Windy City "Double Newark" years ago.

"Nothing going on," I replied. "I'm taking a vacation. Don't have to get back till September."

This handed him a laugh.

"I'm on the level," I went on. "Got the car waiting in front of the door now."

I'll be right over," he shouted, and ten minutes later we were climbing into the automobile.

"Before we start, I'd like to take a spin as far as Providence and see the old home town," I suggested.

"Anywhere you like, kid," he chuckled. "Go through to 'Frisco if you want to. I'm with you."

"Not a bad idea at that. Let's do it."

"What?"

"Go through to 'Frisco from Providence."

"Say, are you kidding me?" He weighed me up.

"No, I'm dead serious," I assured him. We shook hands; the thing was settled. After the Providence trip we were to start for the Coast.

"See you boys next September," he shouted to a group of Friars in front of the club, and away we went for a "rare old time," as we put it.

We pulled into New Haven about seven o'clock that evening, and stopped at the Taft House for dinner.

"Let's stay here overnight and get an early start in the morning," Reardon suggested while we were dining.

We engaged rooms, left a six o'clock call, and went to our suite to have a smoke and talk over our vacation plans before retiring. During the chat I reached for the telephone, and Reardon pulled it out of my hands.

"Let that alone," he demanded. "If you're going to enjoy this vacation, you've got to keep away from telephones."

"I must ring up the Cohan and Harris Theater, Steve," I explained. "Something I forgot to tell Sam Forrest." Forrest was the Cohan and Harris stage manager.

"Tell him when we get back next September," said Reardon.

"Listen, Steve," I pleaded. "I promise you that after to-night I won't talk over the phone except to my own family for the next two months." He fell for this and handed me the instrument. I put in the call and got a quick connection.

"Hello! How's the house to-night, son?" I was talking to the treasurer in the theater box office.

"Oh, is that you Mr. Cohan. Gosh! We've been trying to locate you for two hours." He seemed terribly excited.

"What's the matter?" I asked.

"Hold the wire a minute," he replied. "Mr. Harris wants to speak to you."

"What's happened, kid," inquired Steve, as he edged closer to the phone.

"I don't know, yet." But I could tell that something was wrong.

"Hello, George!" It was Harris' voice. "Where are you?"

"I'm in New Haven," I answered.

"Well, you're in luck," and he laughed. "There's a riot around this town to-night."

"What do you mean?" I sensed what it was.

"The actors have gone on a strike," he replied.

"Hold the wire a second, Sam." And I turned and told Reardon the news.

He fell over on one of the beds, laughing like a two-year-old.

"There goes our vacation," he shouted.

"See you in the morning, Sam," I yelled to Harris, and hung up the receiver.

It took us until three o'clock to locate the chauffeur. He'd been dismissed for the night. We finally found the young man, and were on our way back to New York at 4.30 in the morning.

"How did you enjoy the trip to California?" I inquired of Reardon as we shot through Bridgeport about six o'clock.

"A delightful trip, Mr. Cohan. A thoroughly delightful trip," he went on. "Still it will seem good to get back to dear old New York again. I dare say the old town's changed considerably since we left for the Coast."

He leaned back in the seat with a funny grin on his face, puffed away at his cigar, and added: "You should have taken this rest years ago, my boy. It's done you the world of good. You look like a new man."

He kept up this line of talk all the way to New York. I wasn't a particularly good audience, however. I had too much on my mind.

CHAPTER XXXII

BATTLING BROADWAY

WE arrived in New York about seven o'clock in the morning, and went to the club for coffee and rolls.

The morning papers all carried front-page stories of the actors' strike, and besides, we gathered enough inside information from the early birds strolling in for breakfast to give us a fairly good idea of the wild and exciting happenings of the night before.

When he'd finished breakfast, Reardon got up from the table and shook hands with me.

"So long, kid," he said. "I'm going home and go to bed for a few weeks' rest. That long trip back from the Pacific coast has tired me out completely." He was still kidding about the vacation. A few minutes later, as I was leaving the club, I heard him saying to the telephone girl:

"You've never been to California? Well, take my tip and make the trip. I wouldn't have missed it for Henry Ford's money." He spent the next few days telling the boys around the club all about the delightful climate.

"Did you see the seals on the rocks?" inquired one fellow who actually believed that Steve had been there.

"Oh yes," answered Reardon, "and I studied them very closely, too."

"What do you mean?" The fellow was interested.

"I mean," said Steve, "that I'm convinced the seals are a 'bunk.' They're made of rubber and are worked by machinery." He had loads of fun with some of the "native son" Friars.

From the club that morning, I went directly to the Cohan and Harris office and waited two hours before any of the staff appeared. About 9.30 Eddie Dunn blew in and told me the full details of the strike. He went on to describe the comical carryings-on of the pickets, soap-box orators, improvised parades, and all of the fireworks, which, he explained, kept up till two o'clock in the morning.

One by one, as the rest of the boys arrived, they related different amusing incidents of the big walk-out and the spectacular manner in which the striking actors celebrated the event.

Not one of the staff seemed to take the thing seriously. They were all having a great laugh and apparently enjoying the "circus."

About eleven o'clock I ran downstairs in the theater, and discovered James Gorman, the stage manager of "The Royal Vagabond" troupe, rehearsing several chorus boys and girls in the principal parts.

"These kids can give a show to-night," he announced as I walked down the aisle.

"They're all anxious to keep working if you'll give them a shot at the thing."

"How did it happen that you chorus people didn't walk out?" I put it up to the boys and girls themselves.

"Nobody asked us to," answered a little blonde as she stepped out of line and down to the footlights.

"Aren't you folks members of the Equity Association?" I asked.

"No. Chorus people are not eligible," explained the little spokesman.

I couldn't get this at all. The striking actors were yelling along the streets that they were fighting for "the little fellow's interest" and still they had walked out and "left the little fellow" flat. It was a paradox.

I don't think the Equity people themselves realized for the moment what they had done. However, they got busy later on and took the chorus into the fold.

"How do the musicians feel about it?" I put the question to Charlie Gebest, my musical director, who was conducting the rehearsal.

"We've had no word of any kind," he replied. "We'll play the show."

"How about the stage crew?" I inquired of the house carpenter, who happened to be standing by at the time.

"Far as we know, everything's all right," he answered.

"Think you can play the piece well enough to keep the curtain up?" I asked the boys and girls.

"Yes, sir." They all shouted at the one time.

"All right. Go ahead and play it." And a cheer went up from the crowd as they danced around the stage with joy.

"We're short two parts; we need two men," said Gorman.

"No, you don't; you need only one," yelled

Sam Forrest as he ran down the aisle. "I'm going to play in that cast." Another cheer from the chorus crowd.

"Well, if that's the way it's going to be, I'll do a little acting myself," I announced, and Forrest and I climbed over the orchestra pit to the stage and joined the company.

We gave what might be called a mighty good "catch as catch can" performance of the piece for the balance of the week to capacity houses. The striking actors gave us many a battle during the time we stayed open, but we battled them right back and stuck on the job. The musicians and stage hands finally walked out and left us no alternative but to close up shop.

Word came to me the second night of the strike that a group of buck dancers were going to kidnap a couple of my chorus boys who had been promoted to principal parts, so from that moment on we never let these kids out of our sight. As a matter of fact, the entire company stuck closely together all the time.

Between matinée and night performances, we'd all dine together.

"Have dinner served for eighty-five people at six-thirty," was the telephone message sent to the Knickerbocker Hotel, and away we'd go, the whole troupe hanging on to one another in fear of abduction, as we'd push our way through the Forty-second Street crowds to the hotel café.

"A banquet every minute." "A million dollars' worth of excitement."

I joined the group of actors opposing the "closed shop" issue, and then the fight was really on.

Some experience. Some education.

Oh, boy! That thing they call human nature has many a twist.

It isn't up to me to write the real story of the actors' strike of 1919.

And even if I did, who would publish it?

"I will," answers the man with the false beard.

"And who are you?"

"Hawkshaw, the detective," cries the member of the council as he tears off his disguise. "How dare you attempt to protect your own interests against the will of the mob," he demands. The whole subject is worthy of a musical review.

When the scrap was over, the theaters open, and the season on, I retired from the firm of Cohan and Harris, and fully intended to take a year's rest. Having already disposed of many of the theatrical properties in which I had been interested, the dissolution was not a difficult matter.

Harris and I parted the same way in which we had first come together—the best of friends—but our partnership of fifteen years had come to an end.

I was determined to keep away from the managerial side of the game from that time on.

About three weeks after my withdrawal from the firm, Steve Reardon said to me:

"On the level, kid, did you quit of your own accord, or were you tipped off to get out before you were thrown out?"

"Where'd you get hold of that idea?" I asked, indignantly.

"Never mind where I got it. Answer the question," he came back.

"I'll answer it right now," I replied. "Come to the telephone with me. I want you to hear what I'm going to say." He followed me to the phone booth.

I rang up the Sam Harris office.

"Hello, Sam! Would you mind if I occupied that vacant office on the third floor of your building?"

"What do you want it for?" inquired Harris.

"I'm going back in the play-producing business," I replied.

I heard Harris laughing over the phone. Reardon fell out of the booth, all but hysterical.

"Sure. It's yours as long as you want it," Harris finally managed to say. I thanked him and hung up.

"Well, old boy," said Reardon, "after this long rest you've had (I'd been out three weeks) you ought to be in great shape to start getting busy again." He started laughing again and kept it up for an hour and a half.

The next morning the sign on the third-floor-front office door in the Harris Building read:

GEORGE M. COHAN PRODUCTIONS

About two o'clock in the afternoon, when I returned from lunch, I had to fight my way through a crowd of actors, actresses, agents, and chorus people that congested the hallways and staircases in search of engagements. When I finally reached my desk, I came face to face with Reardon, who stood there, still laughing away to beat the band.

"Are you going to keep this up all your life?" I asked him. "This is no joke with me. I'm going to show these guys that they can't drive me out of the show game until I'm ready to go."

"Listen, kid, I've got something to tell you," he said between giggles. "Nobody said they had driven you out. I manufactured that idea myself. I knew what you'd do the minute I pulled it on you."

"You mean to say you purposely 'kidded' me back into the business?"

"Sure I did," he answered. "I was afraid you'd go mad without a whole lot of work on your mind."

Harrison Grey Fiske walked in the office at this point and threw a manuscript on my desk.

"There's a darn good play," he said. "Well worth producing."

"All right," I replied. "We'll produce it."

And we did. And it cost me fifty thousand dollars. And Reardon didn't show up for a month.

CHAPTER XXXIII

SHOWMANSHIP

"COHAN better stick to his writing. He'll never make a successful manager." That was the general opinion after the ill-fated production of "Genius and the Crowd," my first single-handed offering.

"We'll see about that," I murmured to myself, and rolled up my sleeves and got busy.

I grabbed a Harbach-Hirsch musical play called "The House That Jack Built," opened it in Washington, where we worked on it day and night for the entire week, changed the title to "Mary," and brought it into Philadelphia the following Monday. Never in the history of Philadelphia theatricals was a bigger hit ever scored than by this little play.

After four weeks of almost unheard-of business, I moved the show to Boston, and for sixteen solid weeks, throughout hot weather and all, broke every Tremont Theater record on the books.

I organized a number two company of "Mary" and sent it on tour. I organized a number three company of "Mary" and sent it on tour. I organized a number four company of "Mary" and sent it on tour. I organized a special company of "Mary" for a return engagement in Boston. It was produced in England, Australia, and every English-speaking country on earth. "Mary" was a million-dollar hit. "Mary" was a riot.

"No use in talking, that guy Cohan's a great showman." All the wiseacres had "turned turtle" on their earlier opinion of my managerial abilities, which, as I've always maintained, goes to prove that "you're a smart man with all smart people if only you're smart enough to prove to the smart people how smart you are." At any rate, I'd waited so long to hear the showmen admit that I "belonged," it certainly came as pretty good news to me.

My next production was a Cohanization of a manuscript called "The Meanest Man in the World." Another whale of a hit. I personally entered the cast for the New York engagement, and later on handed the part over to Otto Kruger.

I next turned my attention to a Cora Dick Gantt play called "The Choice of the Superman."

"I'll give these babies something to talk about," I thought to myself, as I sprinkled the Cohan salt and pepper all over the 'script and poked fun at a serious effort.

I called it "The Tavern" and opened the piece at the Cohan Theater.

Help! Murder! Police! Fire!

Another panic was on.

"Somebody stop this man," the literary ladies and gentlemen again demanded. The bold, bad band of dramatic critics drew forth their sharpened pencils and stabbed me to the heart.

"What's it all about?"

"What's he trying to do?"

"Where's the plot?"

"What's the idea?"

"What's all the business for?" they cried, as they watched the crowds piling into the Cohan Theater.

"What's all the shootin' for?" the low comedian of the play would shout back at them during each performance.

The public flocked to "The Tavern," and to

this day I still believe that it was sheer curiosity that brought the crowds to see for themselves whether or not any play could possibly be as bad as the New York critics had declared this one.

A second company, organized and sent to Chicago, duplicated the New York hit, and before the season ended, "The Tavern" was the most widely discussed and best advertised play in America.

I now came along with another Harbach-Hirsch musical piece, "The O'Brien Girl." Bang! Another bull's-eye hit. Eighteen capacity weeks in Boston before the New York engagement, a number two company on tour, and just getting ready to organize the number three, when the Equity Association declared "closed shop" on all independent managers.

Rather than submit to this ruling, I closed my attractions (I had twelve shows in operation that season), sent them to the storehouse, dismantled my business offices, hopped on a boat and went to England, and laid plans for several London productions.

In two weeks' time I was set and ready to try my luck as an English producer, and jumped back to New York to engage certain actors for certain parts. I had booked return passage and was to sail again for England within the week.

A committee of independent actors, headed by Henry Miller and Otis Skinner, called on me and requested that I reconsider my decision to produce abroad. Henry Miller, as president of the "open shop" actors' association, spoke for the entire membership.

"We don't want you to go," he said, and presented me with a resolution signed by every man and woman of his organization.

"All right, Mr. Miller. If they feel that way about it, that's the way it's going to be." There was nothing else to say.

I immediately rejoined the Producing Managers Association and cabled to London that all bets were off. I opened up my offices, got the staff busy on the job, hurried down to Atlantic City with a couple of stenographers, had a piano shoved into my apartments, and returned to New York in three weeks with a new Cohan musical play, entitled "Little Nellie Kelly."

CHAPTER XXXIV

SUMMING UP

I PRODUCED "Little Nellie Kelly" at the Tremont Theater in Boston, where, after a run of sixteen weeks, it had broken all house records. Even "Mary" and "The O'Brien Girl" were "also-rans" in the matter of receipts and popularity. Four big song hits in the play, and altogether my biggest musical-comedy success since the days of "Little Johnny Jones." A second company was organized and presented the piece on tour, while the original cast held on for a solid year's run at the Liberty Theater in New York City.

With this piece successfully running, I grabbed hold of a manuscript of a comedy called "How Very American," by Arthur Goodrich; the result was "So This Is London!" This little farce, after being properly "panned" and roasted by almost every one of the Broadway critics, blossomed into one of the greatest American comedy hits of all time. Number two and three companies toured the United States, while the original cast continued its New York run at the Hudson Theater for fifty consecutive weeks before moving to Boston and Philadelphia.

"So This Is London!" was also a huge success in the city of London, where for forty-odd weeks the English public flocked to the Prince of Wales Theater and laughed as heartily at the piece as American audiences ever did.

During the London run of this play, I also produced "Little Nellie Kelly" in the English metropolis, where it duplicated, for an entire season, its New York hit at the New Oxford Theater.

I followed this up with still another Cohan musical play, called "The Rise of Rosie O'Reilly," which divided a solid year between Boston, New York, Philadelphia, and Chicago; at this writing it is in rehearsals for an Australian production.

I next gave my attention to straight comedy again and turned out an original character study entitled "The Song and Dance Man." After fifteen weeks of a road tour, I finally brought the piece into the Hudson Theater, appearing personally in the title rôle.

And now comes the big laugh of the story—the real punch to the tale. The actors admitted that I was a *good actor.* Gosh darn it! Why did they keep me waiting so long?

Well, anyway, at last I'd come into my own. My dreams had all come true. My highest ambition satisfied at last. Hurrah! I'm a good actor.

Well, it's been a great life, boys.

"A charmed life," say my friends.

"A lucky life," say others.

They may be right at that.

I'm not saying that I haven't been lucky.

As a matter of fact, I consider myself lucky to have come out of it all alive.

But don't forget, dear reader, that since 1904, when I first peeked in on Broadway with my "Johnny Jones" hat and dandy little cane, I have had to go some to keep up with the mad procession.

In the past twenty years I have written, signed, and produced thirty-one plays of my own.

Besides this, I have collaborated with other authors on fourteen plays to which my name was never attached as co-author. Forty-five plays in twenty years' time is no job for a lazy man, old top.

Writing and composing five hundred songs and musical numbers (conservatively) in the same space of time is also not any particular pastime or recreation.

Producing, owning, controlling, and being interested actively and financially in the presentation of a hundred and twenty-eight theatrical attractions is hardly what might be called a "cinch."

Presenting, featuring, managing, and being interested in the business direction of such stars as Mrs. Fiske, Fay Bainter, Mary Ryan, Arnold Daly, E. J. Dodson, Leo Ditrichstein, Chauncey Olcott, Thomas E. Shea, William Collier, Richard Carle, Lawrence D'Orsay, Wallace Eddinger, Douglas Fairbanks, Frank Bacon, John Barrymore, Victore Moore, Gertrude Hoffman, Lowell Sherman, Robert Hilliard, Edith Day, Donald Brian, Nora Bayes, Elizabeth Hines, Fred Niblo, George (Honey Boy) Evans, Fritzi Scheff, Julian Eltinge, Laurette Taylor, Grant Mitchell, and a thousand lesser lights, isn't the softest proposition that a lucky bird ever fell heir to.

Buying, selling, and juggling around controlling interests of various big city theaters is not altogether a child's occupation.

No, sir. The real answer is work, work, and lots of it—and plenty of speed, too, kid. Don't forget the speed.

With all my other activities of the past twenty years as a Broadway showman, I have also found time to personally appear in my own plays 428 weeks, 3,471 performances. This does not include at least two hundred testimonial and benefit performances.

And so I sing:

" 'Tisn't easy to say, Good-by, Broadway,
After years of hanging 'round you night and day.
'Tisn't easy to go, and I want you to know
It's all been fun for me. What you've done for me
Oh, I know I could never repay.
But wherever I stray, from you, Broadway,
Every night I'm going to kneel right down and pray
That your lights keep shining bright
Brighter every night,
'Tisn't easy to say, Good-by, Broadway."

And now, just a word in closing to all aspiring young playwrights.

My theory of popular playwriting and the way to set about it is, very briefly, as follows:

First, think of something to say. Then say it the way the theatergoer wants to hear it said, meaning, of course, that you must lie like the dickens.

I expect the same rule holds good in most any form of story-writing, and, as I have stuck to truth and nothing but the truth, with no attempt at dramatization, I dare say this mess of words has been about as interesting as a Chinese conversation. If I've guessed right, don't worry. I forgive you.

With these few remarks, I now wish to announce my immediate and permanent retirement from the literary field.

> "And so he snuck off, all alone by himself, and nobody didn't see him no more."
>
> ——PECK'S BAD BOY.

CURTAIN